THE NORA NOTEBOOKS

THE TROUBLE WITH BABIES

Also by Claudia Mills

The Nora Notebooks: The Trouble with Ants

THE NORA NOTEBOOKS

THE TROUBLE WITH BABIES

Book 2

CLAUDIA MILLS

Illustrated by Katie Kath

Alfred A. Knopf · New York

THIS IS A BORZOI BOOK PUBLISHED BY ALFRED A. KNOPF

All rights reserved. Published in the United States by Alfred A. Knopf, an imprint of Random House Children's Books, a division of Penguin Random House LLC, New York.

Knopf, Borzoi Books, and the colophon are registered trademarks of Penguin Random House LLC.

Visit us on the Web! randomhousekids.com

Educators and librarians, for a variety of teaching tools, visit us at RHTeachersLibrarians.com

Library of Congress Cataloging-in-Publication Data is available upon request. ISBN 978-0-385-39165-8 (trade) — ISBN 978-0-385-39166-5 (lib. bdg.) — ISBN 978-0-385-39168-9 (ebook)

The text of this book is set in 12.5-point New Aster.

Printed in the United States of America
August 2016
10 9 8 7 6 5 4 3 2 1

First Edition

To Kataleya Lee Wahl,
my favorite baby in the whole world

-C.M.

Nora Alpers didn't believe in luck. She believed in the laws of science, which left no room for luck, good or bad. But right now, on this Wednesday morning in March, she felt as if either luck or the laws of science had turned against her. Otherwise, she wouldn't be stuck with Emma Averill as her science-lab partner.

"What if we get electrocuted?" Emma wailed as Nora prepared to connect one end of a copper wire to the positive terminal of their dry-cell battery.

"We won't," Nora said, trying to keep her voice even.

"We could," Emma shot back. "This is exactly how people get electrocuted—by doing dangerous things with electricity."

"This isn't dangerous!" So much for keeping an even tone. "No one in the history of the world has ever been electrocuted by a ten-volt battery."

"Well, I don't want to be the first!"

Nora sighed. She didn't mind doing the experiment all by herself; in fact, she preferred it. And Emma was a nice enough person, one of the friendliest girls in their fourth-grade class. But Nora was tired of explaining to Emma that they weren't going to receive a fatal shock by sitting two feet away from a low-voltage battery.

"I hate electricity," Emma moaned.

"You use electricity to charge your phone," Nora said.

This was the same phone on which Emma showed the other girls countless videos of her cat, Precious Cupcake. Nora's own pets, a few dozen ants in her ant farm, were as different from Precious Cupcake as pets could be.

"You use electricity for . . ." Nora tried to think of another of Emma's favorite electric-powered gadgets. "For your hair dryer." Emma's golden curls obviously benefited from electric-powered hair-styling equipment, unlike Nora's straight brown hair, which dried by itself without any electrical assistance.

"My cousin knows someone who had a friend who had a neighbor who was electrocuted when her hair dryer fell into the bathtub," Emma said triumphantly, as if this were reason to avoid touching any wire in any science lab ever.

Nora sighed again.

Across the room, her friend Amy Talia was busily working away with Anthony Tobias, a pleasantly serious boy who played the violin. Both of them were managing to hook up a wire to a battery without any fuss.

On the other side of the room, Mason Dixon and Brody Baxter were working happily together. Somehow these two best friends had ended up in the same pod and had gotten to be science partners, too. Talk about luck! In the back of the room, Dunk Edwards was working with Sheng Ji, who had to be the unluckiest boy of all for ending up with Dunk as his science partner. At this moment, Dunk was poking a stray wire into Sheng's somewhat chubby middle.

"Is Dunk electrocuting Sheng?" Emma asked nervously.

"The wire isn't even connected to anything," Nora pointed out. "It's not conducting any electricity at all."

Reassured, Emma giggled appreciatively at Dunk's antics.

"Dunk!" Coach Joe called over to Dunk's pod.

Coach Joe wasn't a coach; he was their usually good-natured teacher who loved anything to do with sports the same way Nora loved anything to do with science.

Nora continued with the experiment, glad that Emma was distracted by watching Dunk redden under Coach Joe's reprimand. Then Dunk poked the wire into Sheng's tummy again, provoking more of Emma's giggles.

At least Nora would be able to do her science-fair project all by herself. March was science-fair month at Plainfield Elementary School, so it was

Nora's favorite month of the school year. Now she had the delicious task of trying to decide what her project would be.

The obvious choice would be to do something involving the ants in her ant farm, but Nora had already done so many ant farm experiments over the past few months that she was ready for a change. Maybe her ants were ready for a change, too. Nora didn't want them to live out their relatively short life spans as nothing but subjects of scientific experimentation.

After a few more minutes, Nora had completed the dry-cell battery experiment and written down the results in her science notebook. Nora loved notebooks: she loved having all her data neatly cataloged there, a record of her findings to save for the rest of the school year. Emma, who had done nothing on the experiment at all, copied everything Nora had written into her own notebook, which had a pink cover featuring a photo of a white kitten with an even pinker bow in its fur. Coach Joe had posted Dunk's name on the chalkboard list labeled "Benched!" so Dunk was sulking. Science time was over.

"Huddle!" Coach Joe called out.

That was his word for an all-class meeting on the football-shaped rug in one corner of the classroom. Nora and Amy found seats on the floor next to Mason and Brody.

"I think our battery was a dud," Mason said. "But then Coach Joe came over and made it work, so maybe *we* were the duds."

"Or maybe Coach Joe is a battery genius," Brody said.

Mason and Brody were inseparable even though they were complete opposites in personality. Mason always saw the glass as half empty; Brody saw it as half full. No, Nora thought: Mason saw the glass as bone-dry, and Brody saw it as overflowing. She herself was the kind of person who would want to measure the volume of water in the glass—in milliliters, of course, not ounces, because true scientists used the metric system—before coming to any conclusions about it.

"Science fair!" Coach Joe said once everyone was seated in the huddle, except for a scowling Dunk, who was still "benched" back at his desk in his pod.

Nora turned her full attention to her teacher.

"This year there are going to be a couple of differences from how you've done the science fair in the past," Coach Joe began.

Nora wished she had brought her science notebook to the huddle so that she could take notes.

"Change number one," Coach Joe said. "In the lower grades, the science fair was optional. You could choose whether to take a turn at bat or not."

Nora had always done the science fair, but most of her classmates, including Amy, hadn't.

"This year it's mandatory. *All* of you are going to be working on a project to display at the fair two weeks from this Friday."

Brody's face brightened. Brody liked to do everything, although Nora couldn't remember whether he had done a science-fair project in third grade or not.

Mason's face darkened. Mason never liked doing anything.

Pouting, Emma raised her hand. "I don't think that's fair. Some people like science, and some people don't. People who like science should get to do the science fair. And people who don't like science shouldn't have to."

"In life, Emma," Coach Joe said, "sometimes we have to do things we don't want to do."

Nora knew that Emma was the kind of girl who almost never had to do anything she didn't want to do.

"In any case," Coach Joe went on, "all of the fourth-grade teachers are in agreement on this one. And we're in agreement on the second big change as well."

Nora waited to hear what he said next.

"In the past, we've seen a lot of amazing science-fair projects."

In all modesty, Nora thought her own science-fair projects had been pretty amazing, especially her third-grade project testing water quality from the creek that ran through the open space at the back of her house. It had won a blue ribbon at Plainfield Elementary and was one of the four projects from her grade selected to go on to the regional science fair.

"But," Coach Joe said, "some of the projects have been *too* amazing."

How could *any* science be too amazing? *All* of science was amazing when you let yourself think about it, which Nora did often.

"So amazing," Coach Joe continued, "that the Plainfield Elementary *student* science fair was starting to seem more like the Plainfield Elementary *parent* science fair."

Nora bristled. Her parents were both scientists, her nineteen-year-old brother was studying science right now at MIT, and her twenty-four-year-old sister was a scientist, too, although she was about to take off time from work to have a baby, due any day.

In preparation for being a ten-year-old aunt, Nora had started writing down baby-related facts in another special notebook she kept at home, where she saved fascinating information about ants and other marvels of the world. Now she was concentrating on finding facts about babies, like the statistic that a baby was born somewhere in the United States every eight seconds. Her father had told her that one.

But none of Nora's scientist relatives had helped her with the science fair one little bit. She had done every project all by herself. Grown-ups never believed that kids could do awesome things without their help.

On the other hand, Nora did remember a couple

of projects by kids in her class that looked as if they had been done mainly by their parents, like Dunk's beautifully presented research on the effect of different materials on a magnetic field. *Dunk* had done *that*?

"So this year," Coach Joe said, "we're not going to be doing our science-fair projects at home with our parents. We'll be doing them here at school. Of course, you may need to do some parts outside of the classroom for practical reasons, but we expect you to work without parental assistance."

That was completely fine with Nora.

"And," Coach Joe continued, "each of you will be working with a partner."

Nora's heart sank.

But it would be all right if she could work with Amy. Amy didn't love science as much as Nora did—few people loved science as much as Nora did—but Amy wanted to be a vet when she grew up, and she was wild about animals. Nora wouldn't mind doing a project on animal behavior with Amy. Nora's parents were always telling her that science was collaborative. That meant that scientists cooperated with one another to achieve their results. Most grown-up scientists conducted their experiments in huge labs with lots of other people, not alone in their own houses.

Nora looked over at Amy. Amy's eyes met hers with the same question. Nora answered it with a big grin, which Amy returned.

The Nora-Amy team would be unbeatable! With Amy as her partner, Nora would be sure to be picked for the regional science fair again this year.

"Because you'll be doing your science-fair projects here at school during our science time," Coach Joe went on to explain, "it will be easiest if you work with your current science partner."

No!

Nora would have to work with *Emma*?

Mason and Brody were already high-fiving each other.

Amy and Anthony exchanged smiles. Anthony would be a good second-best choice as a partner for Amy. But as a partner for Nora, Emma would be the worst choice in the world!

Nora wanted to raise her hand in protest, echoing Emma's comment from five minutes ago: "I don't think that's fair!"

But she knew already what Coach Joe would say in reply: "In life, Nora, sometimes we have to do things we don't want to do."

Maybe Nora should start believing in luck.

Because right now her luck was terrible.

Approximately 130 million babies are born each year. That means that 4 babies are born in the world every <u>second</u>. A baby is going to be born in my family very soon. But I hope it's not today. I have enough else to worry about right now!

2

As soon as Nora got home after school the next day, she could hear her mother talking on her cell phone. Nora's parents were both professors at the university. Her mother was an astrophysicist, studying the rings of Saturn. Her father was a biochemist, studying extremely tiny molecules with extremely long names. But they worked in their home offices a lot, too.

Nora and Emma hadn't talked yet about the science fair; they wouldn't have science time in school again until tomorrow, Friday. But Emma certainly hadn't squealed with rapture at the thought of being Nora's partner, either.

"How far apart are they?" Nora's mother said into the phone.

How far apart were what?

"Ten minutes?" her mother said. "Have you called your doctor? What did she say?"

Nora's mother waved hello to her in a distracted way, mouthing the word *Sarah*.

Nora should have guessed that her mother was talking to her sister about the baby, the baby, the baby. *When the baby comes* had become her mother's favorite expression. It was fast becoming Nora's least favorite expression.

When the baby comes, Sarah and the baby were going to stay at Nora's house for a few weeks because Sarah's husband, Jeff, was away on active duty as an air force pilot.

When the baby comes, Nora was going to become Aunt Nora. She liked the grown-up sound of her new name. And it was pleasing that someone who studied the *a-n-t* was also going to be an *a-u-n-t*. But she didn't know anything about how to take care of babies, and surely an aunt shouldn't be as

15

clueless about babies as . . . as Emma was about batteries. But maybe some of the facts she was collecting about babies to write in her fascinating-facts notebook would come in handy.

When the baby comes, they were going to find out whether it was a boy or a girl. Sarah and Jeff still didn't know; they didn't *want* to know. That seemed ridiculous to Nora. If something was knowable, if all the doctors and nurses knew it, why would you want to be the only ignorant one? Nora wanted to know everything that could be known in the entire universe.

"I want it to be a surprise" was all Sarah would say.

Nora tuned back in to what her mother was saying on her end of the conversation.

"Yes . . . yes . . . Definitely . . . I'll meet you at the birthing center as soon as I can get there." Sarah lived about an hour's drive away. "All right . . . Oh, sweetie . . . I'm leaving now."

Clicking off the phone, her mother gave Nora a shaky smile.

"She's starting to have contractions. Her doctor said to go to the hospital. So I'm heading there now. I'll text Amy's mom to see if you can stay with Amy until your dad finishes work. He has a late meeting."

Nora liked spending time at Amy's house, with Amy's extensive menagerie: two dogs, two cats, two rabbits, and two parakeets. But she also thought she'd be fine at home by herself with her ants for company. Somebody who was about to become Aunt Nora could surely stay at home alone for an hour or two. But her mother was a worrier.

"Oh, Nora!" Her mother caught her up in a hug. "The baby is on its way! And when he or she gets here, our lives are going to be changed forever!"

Nora wasn't sure she liked the sound of that at all.

Nora checked on her ants, giving them one small piece of celery to keep them busy while she was gone. Then she shrugged on her homework-filled backpack and walked over to Amy's house, a few blocks away.

Amy's big dog, Woofer, and her little dog,

Tweeter, jumped up on Nora when Amy answered the door, and her cats, Mush Ball and Snookers, meowed around her ankles. Just about the only kind of creature Amy didn't love happened to be ants.

"So the baby's almost here," Amy's mother, Mrs. Talia, said, shooing the dogs away as she came into the front hall to greet Nora. "Did they find out yet if it's a boy or a girl?"

Nora shook her head.

"I think that's refreshing," Amy's mother said. "Keep some room in life for mystery."

Nora and Amy exchanged glances. The whole point of being an ant scientist or a veterinarian was to solve mysteries, not to make room for even more of them.

"What are you hoping for, a niece or a nephew?" Amy's mom asked.

Nora already knew what to say in reply, because she had heard Sarah say it so often. "Just a healthy baby."

Amy's mother smiled. "Well, you'll be one of the youngest aunts at Plainfield Elementary School, that's for sure."

Amy, who liked to putter in the kitchen, fixed a special snack in Nora's honor called "ants on a log." The logs were stalks of celery filled with peanut butter. The ants were raisins stuck on top. After gobbling them up, the girls settled themselves cozily on the couch in the family room. It was strange to be doing such ordinary things when a new niece or nephew was getting ready to be born.

Mrs. Talia came by with an update from Nora's mom. "It's all moving along, much faster than the doctor expected."

"That's good," Nora said. She assumed it was good, since Amy's mom sounded pleased.

"How did Sarah prepare the nursery without knowing the sex?" Amy's mom asked. "It's so hard to find anything for babies that isn't pink or blue."

Nora shrugged. Surely there had to be some baby decorations that were yellow or green or orange or purple. While she didn't particularly mind pink, it was bizarre how people thought that every girl on earth wanted to live surrounded by over-whelming pinkness. *No* girl Nora knew wanted to have *everything* in her life pink.

Well, no girl except for Emma.

Thinking of Emma made Nora remember the science fair.

"Have you and Anthony come up with a science-fair idea yet?" she asked Amy.

"We can't decide whether to do something about animals for me, like testing rabbits' sense of smell, or something about music for him, like figuring out why different strings on the violin make different sounds."

Both ideas sounded better to Nora than anything she and Emma were likely to come up with. What would Emma consider a truly great science-fair idea? How to measure the cuteness of a cat? How long a cat would be willing to wear a silly outfit? How to get a cat to sit still for endless cat photographs?

How on earth were she and Emma going to be able to agree on anything?

But Nora wasn't going to let the science fair be ruined this year. She wasn't!

Maybe . . . if Emma liked cats so much because of their cuteness, it was possible she also liked babies. Lots of people thought babies were cute. The two of them could study the science of newborn babies: how they reacted to heat, to light, to sound. Nora had already figured out all those things about the ants in her ant farm. Now she could find out how a human baby compared to ants.

If she had to have Emma as a science-fair partner, and had to have a new niece or nephew living in her house, maybe she could do both things together and make it all work out somehow.

Nora ended up staying at Amy's house for dinner. The girls helped Amy's parents prepare all the fixings for make-your-own burritos, as Amy's second-grade brother, Sheridan, swiped pieces of tomato and avocado as fast as they could chop them. With the dogs and cats underfoot, it was definitely different from Nora's quiet, peaceful house. Though maybe her house wasn't going to be quiet and peaceful for much longer.

When dinner was over, just as Nora was helping clear the table, Amy's mother's cell phone rang. She handed it to Nora, beaming. "It's for you!"

Nora held the phone to her ear.

"Oh, honey," her mother said, "Sarah had a healthy seven-pound, eight-ounce beautiful baby girl! She's tired. Both of them are tired—being born is hard work! But mother and baby are doing great. I wanted you to be the first to know."

Now there was a tiny new person existing in the world, and not just in the world, but in Nora's own family.

That was an amazing thought.

"Does she have a name?" Nora asked.

"Nellie," her mother replied. "Nellie Suzanne. Aunt Nora and Niece Nellie—they sound good together, don't you think? I'll be home later tonight. But for now, start celebrating!"

So Nora had become Aunt Nora, with a brand-new baby niece.

A niece who was soon to help her earn a blue ribbon at the Plainfield Elementary science fair.

Blue, not pink.

Nellie was born on Thursday, but the most common day to be born in the United States is Tuesday. This is one of the strangest facts I have ever read. Why would a baby know or care what day of the week it is? Nellie was born in March, but the most common month to be born is August. So far, Nellie isn't acting like a common baby, except for her weight. The average birth weight is 7.5 pounds, and that's exactly what Nellie weighed.

"You and your partner can start brainstorming your science-fair ideas," Coach Joe told the class the next day at the start of science time.

Nora looked at Emma.

Emma looked at Nora.

Nora made herself wait for Emma to break the silence. She knew she had a tendency to be out-spoken when it came to science, and Coach Joe had told the class that he wanted both partners to contribute equally to the project in every way.

After a long moment, Emma lifted her chin.

"Nothing to do with ants," she said.

Nora had already decided she was going to give her ants a rest, but Emma's negativity about them made her bristle.

"Nothing to do with cats," Nora shot back.

Emma adjusted the pink bow in her curly blond hair. Emma was always fussing with her hair or her clothes; Nora had absolutely no interest in either.

"Nothing to do with electricity," Emma said.

Nothing to do with pinkness, Nora wanted to retort. If she didn't speak up soon enough, Emma would want to display their results on a pink poster board, or at least write them on a white poster board with a pink marker. But Nora wasn't going to let the conversation get any more ridiculous than it was already. It was time to stop talking about what they *weren't* going to do and to start talking about what they *were.*

"I was thinking," Nora said. "My older sister just had a baby—last night, in fact—and—"

Emma squealed so loudly that kids at other pods turned around to look.

"Ohhhh!" Emma closed her eyes and clasped

her hands against her chest. "I looooove babies! Don't you?"

Nora hadn't seen her new niece yet. Sarah and Nellie were coming home from the hospital to-morrow, Saturday. So Nora had no idea if she was going to looooove babies.

She might.

Or she might not.

"Is it a boy or a girl?"

Nora had known that would be the first thing Emma would ask. It was strange how important everyone thought that was, as if everything about the rest of your life hung on whether you were born a male or a female. Nora and Amy had more in common with Mason and Brody than they did with Emma. A *lot* more.

"A girl," Nora answered. "Nellie."

"Ohhh! I looooove her name!"

Maybe Emma's rapture over babies in general, and Nellie in particular, was a good sign that Emma would also like the idea of studying how newborns reacted to heat, light, and sound. Well, how *one* newborn reacted. That was a problem with their project. You couldn't really prove anything about *all* babies by studying *one* baby. Still, one baby was a start.

"So," Nora pressed on, "Nellie's going to be staying at my house for a while, and I thought maybe you could come over—"

"Yes! Like, tomorrow? Could I come over tomorrow?"

"Well . . ." Nora thought for a minute. Sarah might need a day or two to get Nellie settled before the scientists arrived with their notebooks. "I should check first with my sister. And I should probably ask her, you know, if she's okay with our doing all of this."

"Our doing all of what?"

Nora had forgotten to tell Emma the full plan.

"The science fair! Doing our project on Nellie. How she reacts to different stimuli. Things like light, heat, sound."

Emma stared at Nora. Plainly Emma didn't get it.

Nora tried to explain more clearly. "Like, how will her behavior change if we put her in a dark room or a bright room? Or a warm room or a cold room?"

Emma still sat, staring.

"I already tested all those things on my ants," Nora said. "Now we can test them on a baby."

Emma found her voice. "A baby is . . . Nora, you can't. . . . It's not the same. . . . Babies are not like ants!"

That was precisely what the science-fair project was supposed to show: *Were* babies like ants or not? But Nora could see that Emma wasn't on board with the project.

Nora had been right the first time. Working together with Emma on the science fair was going to be impossible.

At lunch, as soon as the girls—Emma, Bethy, Elise, Tamara, Amy, and Nora—were seated at their usual table, Emma announced that Nora was a brand-new aunt of a brand-new niece.

The other girls—except for Amy, who already knew every detail—reacted to this news the way they always reacted when Emma showed them endless videos of Precious Cupcake on her cell phone. Emma somehow seemed to bring out squealing and gushing in all who surrounded her.

"Awww!" said Bethy.

"I love her name!" said Elise.

"You're Aunt Nora!" said Tamara.

"Do you have any pictures?" Emma asked.

"When can we see her?" a chorus of voices asked all at once.

"Soon," Nora promised.

"Like, how soon?" Emma demanded.

"We want to see her when she's teeny-tiny," Bethy chimed in.

"Like, this weekend?" Emma asked.

"She's not even home yet," Nora protested.

"Well, as soon as she gets home," Emma persisted.

Nora smiled weakly. She hoped Sarah would let her host a baby-viewing party, as Emma was clearly going to give her no peace until she did.

"Can we hold her?"

"Can we change her clothes?"

"Can we feed her?"

Nora gave Amy a puzzled look. Amy returned a good-natured shrug, but she tugged on her short, perky braid the way she did when she was excited about something, and her eyes were shining.

Who could have guessed that having your sister give birth to an ordinary human baby could turn you into an instant lunch-table celebrity?

Lunch was followed by another class huddle, this time to explain the next social-studies project. Nora wished they could spend March focusing on the science fair. Well, she had wished that before she had found herself partnered with Emma. It was too much to have a big social-studies project to work on, too. But Coach Joe thought they had to study other things at school besides science.

"Team," Coach Joe said once he had everybody's attention. "We are about to head west."

Nora read bewilderment on her classmates' faces. She wasn't sure herself what Coach Joe was going to say next.

"Our American colonists have a brand-new country now," Coach Joe went on. "We've seen them win the American Revolution. We've seen them hammer out their Constitution. But now their brand-new country is starting to feel small and cramped. Thomas Jefferson sent Meriwether

Lewis and William Clark all the way to Oregon to explore new land for settlement. And now, team, *you* are all going to be heading out west on the Oregon Trail, traveling over two thousand miles, from Missouri to Oregon, by covered wagon."

Emma raised her hand. "Is this going to be a class trip?"

"It's going to be a class trip taken during the year 1846, at the height of the trail's use by westward-bound pioneers. A class trip taken with our imaginations."

Nora didn't like the sound of that. She wasn't as good with imagination as she was with reality.

Coach Joe produced two stacks of index cards, each bound together with a rubber band.

"These are your fate cards," he said, holding up a stack in each hand.

Nora liked the sound of that even less. *Fate* was a woo-woo word. People who believed in fate were the same people who believed in luck. They were the people who read their horoscope every day in the newspaper or had some old lady with gold hoop earrings tell their fortune by studying the lines in the palm of their hand. Nora would never do either of those things.

"Each card," Coach Joe continued, "contains a name of some pioneer on the Oregon Trail. A name and a *destiny*."

Another woo-woo word.

"I'm going to hold these out, facedown, and each of you will pick a card. And then, drawing on the reading you'll be doing in our textbook and the material I'll be sharing with you in class, you're going to write a diary for that person."

"How long does it have to be?" Dunk asked.

"You can make it as *long* as you want," Coach Joe said, with a twinkle in his eye. "But the *shortest* it can be is four entries, one page each, spread out over the time your character spends on the trail."

At the thought of writing four whole diary entries, Dunk stabbed himself in the chest with an imaginary dagger.

Emma giggled.

Mason asked the next question. "So what kinds of things happen to these people?" Nora could tell that Mason was already envisioning the hideously bad things that were going to happen to *him*.

"All kinds of things," Coach Joe replied. "One of you will die on the trail from a disease called cholera. One of you will drown crossing a raging river. One of you will be bitten by a rattlesnake."

"All three will happen to me," Mason whispered to Nora and Brody with gloomy satisfaction. "I'll get bitten by a snake, and then I'll get cholera, and then I'll drown. What do you want to bet?"

"One of you will be killed in an Indian raid. The Native Americans, who owned this land first, weren't pleased, to say the least, to have *their* land sold to Thomas Jefferson by the king of France."

"Does anything good happen to anybody?" Brody asked.

"Sure. You might give birth to a baby on the trail."

More giggles from Emma, echoed by giggles from Bethy, Tamara, and Elise.

"And some of you will get all the way to the fertile valleys of Oregon and settle down to a long and happy life."

Brody's face lit up. If anyone was going to live a long and happy life, it had to be Brody.

Nora had a question of her own now.

"Why are there two decks of cards?" she asked. But she already knew the answer.

"One deck has fate cards for boys, and one for girls," Coach Joe told her.

Nora supposed she should be grateful that at least the cards weren't blue and pink.

"All right," Coach Joe said. "Let's begin. The moment has come for each of you pioneers to find out your fate."

Boy babies are on average 4 or 5 ounces heavier and half an inch longer at birth than girls. This means boy babies have a harder time being born. So maybe that is one way that being a male or a female does matter right from the start?

Dunk grabbed his card first. He seemed to think that the person who chose first had the best chance of getting a good fate. But Nora knew that wasn't true. With thirteen cards in the boys' deck, each boy had a one-in-thirteen chance at each fate, whatever order the cards were chosen.

"I'm Tom Talbot," Dunk announced, staring down at his card. "It says that I'm married to Martha Talbot, and I have three kids. I make it all the way to Oregon and set up a general store. I bet I earn a ton of money selling stuff to the rest of you. I'll be rich, suckers!" He smirked, obviously as pleased with himself as if he had survived the Oregon Trail and reaped a fortune in real life.

"Good for you, Tom Talbot," Coach Joe said. "But remember, the point of the assignment isn't what happens to your *character*, but what *you* write about it in your *diary*."

Dunk's face fell. Plainly, he had forgotten that part.

Emma's best friend, Bethy, chose the first card from the girls' deck.

"My husband gets shot and killed in an Indian raid, and I crush my leg in a wagon accident. Great!" Bethy moaned.

"Sometimes the worst fates make the best diaries," Coach Joe told her. "The stories we remember longest, the ones that touch us most deeply, are often the ones without the happy endings. And they definitely aren't stories where everything is happy from start to finish. A story without problems for its main character isn't much of a story at all."

Sheng drew a fate card for being a doctor who helped treat an outbreak of cholera on the trail. He looked pleased.

Amy drew a fate card for being a mother who killed a rattlesnake that was about to attack her children.

"Exciting!" she whispered to Nora. Nora could imagine Amy bravely facing down a rattlesnake, though knowing Amy, she'd probably want to find some way of taming the snake and making it another pet.

Elise's card told her she'd give birth to a baby in Wyoming, a baby who would die a week later. Nora knew Elise, who wanted to be an author, would be glad to have a wrenching tragedy to write about.

Brody's face shone with anticipation as he took his card. Even Nora expected Brody to get a happy fate like Dunk's. Brody was the happiest person in their class. For all Nora knew, Brody might be the happiest person in the world.

"I'm Bill Breeden," Brody read. "I like my name! Two *B*s, just like Brody Baxter. And I have a faithful dog with me! That's like my dog! And then I get to Wyoming! And then—"

His voice broke off.

"And then what?" Dunk asked, clearly hoping the answer would be something terrible.

"Then I die," Brody said. "I get a fever, and I die. I die, and then I'm dead."

Brody sounded so heartbroken that Nora couldn't help feeling sad herself. But she pulled herself together.

"It's just a social-studies project!" she whispered to Brody as Tamara was choosing the next card, taking too long to decide which of the identical-looking, facedown cards to select. "It doesn't really happen! None of these fates really happen!"

"But he even had my same initials," Brody whispered back. "And a dog like mine, too."

Tamara didn't read her card aloud. Coach Joe hadn't said people had to share their fates with the rest of the class. Nora decided she wouldn't share her fate, either.

It was Mason's turn to pick. "If Brody dies of a fever, I'm going to die of a fever, plus twenty Indian arrows in my chest, plus . . . maybe a tornado?"

When Mason looked at his card, he seemed as bewildered as Brody had been.

"I live," Mason said. "I'm Jake Smith, the head of the wagon train, and I get to Oregon, where I have a successful wheat farm. Coach Joe, I think I got the card Brody was supposed to get, and he got the card I was supposed to get."

Coach Joe grinned at Mason. "Sorry, Mason. You're luckier than you thought, my friend. You'll have to make the best of a long life, good health, and prosperity. And, team, no trading fates. What you pick is what you get. That's the whole thing about fate."

Nora was surprised to find her pulse quickening as she got ready to take one of the last cards left in the girls' deck. She forced herself to reach for the closest one.

It's just a social-studies project! It doesn't really matter! None of the fates are real!

Silently she started reading the information typed on her card.

You are Martha Talbot, wife of Tom Talbot.

Tom Talbot! Dunk! She was Dunk's wife!

She skimmed over the rest, about the three children she already had, plus the two more born when she got to Oregon, and how she became a contented shopkeeper's wife.

41

Nora knew there was no way she could have gotten a fate card for being a scientist heading west on the Oregon Trail, studying its flora and fauna—its plants and animals—through the changing terrain. There were hardly any women scientists back then.

But *anything* would be better than being happily married to Dunk!

Emma must have seen Nora's face darken.

"What did you get?" Emma whispered.

While Nora had no intention of reading her horrible card aloud, it seemed silly to refuse to answer Emma's simple question. Wordlessly, she handed her card to Emma.

Emma flushed as she read it, then thrust it back at Nora almost as if she was angry. Angry at Coach Joe for sticking Nora with the worst fate of all?

No. Nora suddenly understood: Emma was angry that Nora had gotten the fate *Emma* wanted. She could so see Emma and Dunk together in their covered wagon—their *pink* covered wagon!

Tom Talbot would do or say something dumb.

"Oh, Tom!" Martha Talbot would giggle.

Coach Joe held up the last girls' card. "Who hasn't picked yet?" He looked around the huddle. "Emma, I guess this fate is for you."

42

Emma snatched the card from Coach Joe's hand, glanced at it, and then put it facedown in her lap.

"All right, pioneers," Coach Joe said, dismissing them. "First diary entry is due on Monday. Get saddled up and ready to ride off on the Oregon Trail."

As the others hurried back to their pods, Emma laid her hand on Nora's arm.

"No one else has seen our cards yet," she whispered. "We could trade, and no one would know."

"What did you get?" Nora asked.

Emma held out her card so Nora could read.

```
You are Ann Whittaker, 26 years old, single.
You are an independent woman heading west
to make your fortune in the new land. You
set up one of the first schools in the Oregon
Territory.
```

Wasn't Nora meant to be Ann Whittaker?
Wasn't Emma meant to be Martha Talbot?
And yet . . .

Coach Joe had told them that they couldn't trade cards to get the fate they wanted. He hadn't let Brody switch his tragic fate for Mason's happy one.

43

Of course, Coach Joe wouldn't know if Emma and Nora quickly, quietly, slipped their cards to each other.

Nora didn't believe in fate any more than she believed in luck. Especially not fates typed up on index cards and handed out for a social-studies assignment.

But even if it hadn't been a direct violation of Coach Joe's rules, it still felt wrong in some strange way to take the fate that belonged to someone else.

She shook her head.

"I'm sorry. Coach Joe said . . . we shouldn't . . . I can't."

"Fine!"

Emma flounced back to their pod, her cheeks blazing.

If it had been impossible to have Emma as her science-fair partner before, what would it be like now that Emma's eyes glittered with rage?

How could Martha Talbot and Ann Whittaker, each one hating her fate, ever manage to work on the science fair together?

When babies are born, they have 300 bones, but when they are grown up, they have only 206 bones. This isn't because some of their bones disappear, but because some of their bones fuse together as they grow.

"They're here!" Nora's mother called from her post by the front window.

Nora's father hurried down from his upstairs office, taking the stairs two at a time.

Feeling suddenly shy, Nora lingered by her ant farm, set on a table in one corner of the family room. It was reassuring to see the ants going about their ordinary antlike business—digging tunnels, carting a morsel of cracker off to a new location— utterly unconcerned with the arrival of the newest human family member.

"Auntie Nora!" her mother called. "Are you coming?"

Nora didn't know why she felt nervous about meeting a two-day-old baby, but for some reason she did. Would people expect her to hold Nellie? What if she dropped her? What were you supposed to do and say around a human being so tiny, so utterly new to the universe?

Her parents had both gone outside to the car to greet Sarah and Nellie. Her father's smile as he carried in Nellie's car seat, with Nellie in it, was even bigger than Brody's biggest grin. Nora had never seen him so excited about anything—not Sarah's college graduation, or her job as a geologist. Not her brother's scholarship to MIT. Not her own blue ribbon at the regional science fair.

And all Nellie had done so far was get herself born!

Nora's mom followed behind, lugging Sarah's suitcase and a diaper bag in one hand and a huge vase of roses in the other. Pink roses, every one of them.

Sarah came last, looking less bulgy than she had when Nora had last seen her, but still a lot rounder than her usual skinny self. She raced over to Nellie's carrier, placed on one cushion of the couch, as if to make sure that Nellie was still in it, alive and breathing.

Nellie was.

Drawing closer, Nora studied her tiny, sound-asleep relative.

She couldn't help but notice that Nellie was bald.

Not completely bald, like an egg, but all that grew on the top of her head was pale, almost invisible fuzz.

Instead of hair, Nellie had a little pink headband with a little pink bow on one side. She was tucked under a little pink blanket. Popped into her mouth was a little pink pacifier.

She was the littlest, pinkest person Nora had ever seen.

"She gets cuter every day!" Nora's mother exclaimed.

Nora refrained from pointing out that two days wasn't a very long time.

Was Nellie cute? Nora didn't think so, but maybe she wasn't the best judge. Would Emma think Nellie was cute? Sarah certainly seemed to. She

hovered over the carrier with adoring eyes. Nora's mother sighed, as if overcome by the magnitude of such extravagant cuteness. Her father was now filming Nellie's cuteness with his video camera, even though the baby had done nothing so far but sleep, and not in a particularly cute or interesting way. What was cute about sleeping?

"I have to hold her," Nora's mother apologized as she unclipped the car-seat harness and lifted Nellie into her arms. Nellie stayed asleep as first Nora's mother and then her father took a turn rocking her.

"Here, Nora," her mother said. "Sit down on the couch, and we'll give her to you."

Nora swallowed hard.

"Maybe later," she said.

She didn't have to hold Nellie *today*. She had the rest of her life to hold Nellie. It didn't have to be today that she tried to act like a real, true aunt to that tiny little bundle.

"Oh, come on," her father said. "You can just sit still while we set her on your lap."

"Um, I just remembered," Nora lied, "that I forgot to feed my ants this morning."

"All right," Nora's mother said, "but hurry back. This is Nellie's big day!"

Nora didn't hurry back, though. She carried her ant farm upstairs to her bedroom and sat for a long while watching the ants do their quiet tunneling. Nora's ants didn't expect her to hold them or say *goo-goo* or *ga-ga* or whatever you were supposed to say to babies. All Nora's ants expected of her was some food and water at regular intervals. She could do that. She could do that perfectly well.

Even though Emma hadn't sounded enthusiastic about doing their science-fair project on Nellie, Nora thought she should check to see if Sarah was on board with it. If the baby's own mother thought that it was a cool idea, how could Emma possibly object?

Of course, all Nellie had done so far was eat and sleep. Even Nora couldn't think of anything scientifically interesting about that. But sooner or later, Nellie was bound to start doing things worth recording in Nora's baby-fact notebook.

Nora waited until her parents had set out

purchased deli salads for lunch and everyone except for Nellie had sat down at the table.

"So," Nora said, in as offhand a way as possible, "my science-fair partner, Emma, and I were talking about possible ideas for our project. We thought we'd like to study something about Nellie. You know, how she reacts to light, heat, sound—things like that."

"You're joking, right?" Sarah asked just as her mom said, "Oh, Nora!" Her father smiled, but that was pretty much what he had been doing nonstop since Nellie was born.

How could a whole family of scientists be so unscientific?

A piercing cry came from the living room.

In a flash, Sarah dashed away from the table, followed by both of Nora's parents. Apparently, it took three human adults to respond to the cry of one human baby. That could be a science-fair project in itself: Why exactly did adult humans respond to newborn babies the way they did?

But the longer Nellie kept on wailing, the more Nora felt herself losing interest in Nellie as a subject of scientific study in any way, shape, or form.

She tried to eat the curried chicken salad and cabbage slaw on her plate, but the crying went on.

And on.

And on.

And on.

By the end of the weekend, Nora knew one definite scientific fact about the behavior of babies.

They cried a lot.

Nellie didn't cry when she was eating, but she had trouble settling down enough to nurse.

She didn't cry when she was sleeping, but she had trouble settling down enough to sleep.

Now Nora knew why people thought sleeping babies were so cute. Sleeping babies were so cute because they weren't crying.

"Do all babies cry so much?" Nora asked Sarah after Nellie finally fell asleep on Sunday afternoon. Nora's father had gone to work at his university office; Nora didn't need to guess why. She, Sarah, and their mother were all in the newly silent family room. Nora had never realized how beautiful silence could be.

Sarah looked offended by the question. "She hardly cries at all!"

If Nellie hardly cried at all, Nora would hate to be around a baby that cried a lot.

"Did I cry when I was a baby?" Nora asked. It was hard to believe she had started out as a squalling, red-faced thing.

"All babies cry," her mother said. "But of my three, I think you cried the least. Or maybe with the third, you don't notice it as much."

"Was I bald when I was a baby?" Nora asked.

Sarah didn't like that question, either.

"Nellie has hair! You just can't see it because it's so blond!"

Or because it's not there.

"You had quite a bit of hair, as I recall," her mother said. "But Sarah's right: dark hair stands out more than light. I have to admit I've forgotten a lot about all of you as babies. Those days go by so fast. Before you know it, you have a toddler, then a kindergartner, then a fourth grader working on her science-fair project. What I do remember most, Nora, is what a one you were for questions. All kids do the *why-why-why* thing until it drives their parents crazy, but with you, I always thought you asked those things because you really wanted to know."

"What kinds of things?"

"'Where do numbers come from?' 'Is there a biggest number?' 'If God made the world, who made God?' 'Can worms think?' 'Can there be a color no one in the world has ever seen before?'"

Nora liked to think of her little-girl self asking questions like that. *Could* there be a color that no one in the world had ever seen before?

Over the baby monitor came a sound that might have been a cat meowing or might have been a baby starting to cry.

Nora's family had no cat.

Sarah jumped up.

"Just wait," Nora's mother told her. "Give her a chance to settle down on her own before you go to her."

Sarah had already started up the stairs.

"Oh well," Nora's mother said. "That's how you are with your firstborn."

Nora looked over fondly at her quiet, quiet ants.

A typical newborn sleeps between 15 and 20 hours a day. If you ask me, a typical newborn cries between 15 and 20 hours a day. But maybe I'm exaggerating? When newborns cry, they don't make any tears because their tear ducts aren't developed yet. But they sure make a lot of noise.

6

It wasn't until Sunday night that Nora remembered that the first entry in their Oregon Trail diary was due on Monday.

With a heavy heart, she carried her ant farm up to her bedroom and sat down at her desk to start thinking about poor Martha Talbot married to awful Tom Talbot—Dunk!—with three children to look after in their cramped covered wagon.

Maybe one of them was a newborn.

A newborn named Nellie who cried a lot.

After all, Nellie was an old-fashioned name that could have belonged to a pioneer baby.

Inspired now, Nora picked up her pen and started writing.

Dear Diary,
    Today we set off from St. Joseph, Missouri, on the Oregon Trail. It is hard being in such a small space with all of us, especially with Nellie, who cries all the time.
    I mean, <u>all</u> the time.
    Because babies are not in fact interesting to write about, contrary to what some people might think, I am going to describe the fascinating mammals, birds, insects, and plants that we see along the trail. I am especially hoping that we might see some ants that are different from the ants in our hometown back in Kentucky.

Nora stopped to think about what to write next. Luckily, she had just finished reading a library book about crows.

In the sky right now, I see a flock of crows. Crows look a lot like ravens because they both

are completely black, but crows have smaller
bills. Crows are highly intelligent. They even use
tools to get food.

After adding a few more crow facts, Nora
checked the length of her diary entry. It was over a
page now. That was more than enough for the first
day of her westward migration.

I hope we see more crows, as well as geese,
beavers, bison, prairie dogs, and, of course,
ants. Now Nellie is crying again—surprise,
surprise. So I must go.
Yours truly,
Martha Talbot

During science time on Monday, Nora waited to
see if Emma had thought of any science-fair ideas
over the weekend. But Emma sat busily doodling
hearts all over her science notebook, as if Nora
wasn't even there.

"So," Nora finally said. "About the science fair?"

"You don't even *like* Dunk!" Emma burst out.

That much was true. But it had nothing whatsoever to do with the science fair. Apparently, Emma was still furious that Nora had refused to trade fates.

"If you don't even like Dunk, how can you be married to him?" Emma asked, her voice rising higher with rage.

"*I'm* not married to Dunk," Nora tried to explain. "*I'm* not married to anybody. The person on my index card is married to Tom Talbot, but I'm not her, and Tom's not Dunk."

Come to think of it, Nora hadn't mentioned Tom Talbot at all in her diary entry. She had filled it with information about crows.

"Anyway," Nora said, as it was clearly time to change the subject. "Nellie's home now, and I talked to my sister, and she said—"

"That we can come over!" Emma finished Nora's sentence for her, a baby-adoring smile replacing her fate-hating scowl. "When? Like, this weekend? Saturday is better for me, but Sunday's okay, too. And Bethy, Elise, and Tamara are all free on Saturday, too. Can you check with Amy?"

"Well, actually . . ."

Nora hadn't yet asked Sarah about having all of her girlfriends over to the house for a Nellie party. What she had been starting to say was that Sarah had nixed the baby project, so they definitely had to think of something else. But it was a relief to have Emma distracted from her disappointment over her fate card.

"I think Saturday will be great," Nora said, desperately hoping that this was true. "Like, at two o'clock?"

"Will she be napping then?" Emma asked.

She'll probably be crying then.

Nora shrugged. "I don't know. I mean, she's only four days old. So I don't know her very well yet. But she's cute when she's sleeping, too."

Or as cute as she ever is.

"I can't wait to tell everybody!" Emma said. "You did bring pictures, didn't you?"

Nora shook her head. "I don't have a cell phone like you do," she apologized. Emma was the only girl in their class who had her own cell phone.

"Well, we'll see her on Saturday anyway."

"So about the science fair," Nora said, now that Emma was finally in a good mood.

"What's it like holding her?" Emma asked. "I've held babies—I have two cousins who are babies—but I didn't get to hold them until they were, like, two months old. I've never held a really tiny baby."

Nora felt herself flushing. "It's okay, I guess."

Nora still hadn't held Nellie yet, but she couldn't make herself tell that to Emma.

Emma came up with more questions. Had Nora given Nellie a bottle yet? Had she helped change her diaper yet? Had she given her a bath yet?

No, no, and no, Nora admitted.

Emma looked surprised. Nora was clearly a disappointment in the aunt department.

"All right, team!" Coach Joe called out. "Science time's over! Get ready to line up for music. Hope you all are closing in on an idea for your project. Let me know if you need any help. I have some books filled with science-fair ideas if anybody's stuck."

Nora filed into line behind Mason and Brody, glad to escape from Emma.

Now it was her turn to be furious. Emma had wasted every single minute of their science time.

They had *no* ideas for the science fair, none at all.

How could Nora, of all people, be stuck on what she loved most?

But she wasn't about to ask Coach Joe for help. Real scientists didn't copy project ideas out of books, ideas for the same old science-fair projects that had been done by millions of kids for centuries—well, for as long as science fairs had existed. The research of real scientists was driven by a burning desire to answer questions they really cared about.

And *not* questions like "What does it feel like to hold a baby?" and "How soon can I come over to your house to hold one?"

Babies can't see color until they are about 4 months old. I wonder how anybody figured that out. It's not like you can ask babies what they see and have them tell you.

"We could do something with model rockets," Nora suggested during science time on Wednesday. She didn't know anything about model rockets, but she'd love an excuse to build one.

Emma shook her head, busy turning the pages of one of Coach Joe's science-fair books, which she had insisted on bringing over to their pod.

"Here's one," Emma said. "'Will a cat prefer homemade or store-bought cat food?'"

"Um . . . I thought we agreed: nothing to do with cats."

Emma flipped through a few more pages.

"Okay, here's another one. 'Does adding salt to water make it boil faster?'"

"Too easy. Too boring."

"Wait," Emma said. "This is a good one. 'What animals are most popular?'"

Really? But it was right there in Coach Joe's book. You got the answer by doing a survey and asking all of your friends which animal they liked best. And that was supposed to count as a science-fair experiment?

"That's not . . . it's not scientific enough," Nora tried to explain.

She took the book from Emma and started searching through it herself. But even the projects that looked more like what Nora thought of as real science—"How do different materials affect air resistance?" "Which metals have greater thermal conductivity?"—didn't excite her. She couldn't bear the idea of doing an experiment that thousands of kids had already done.

"Nora," Emma said, "put the book down. I just had a brilliant idea. A truly brilliant, amazing, fantastic, fabuloso idea."

Nora closed the book, as Emma plainly wasn't going to announce her idea until she did. But she knew there was close to a zero percent chance that she would think any science-fair idea of Emma's was brilliant, amazing, fantastic, and fabuloso.

"Are you ready? Are you sure you're ready?"

"Emma!" Nora could take only so much fanfare.

"We could . . ." Emma paused for effect. "We could . . . test different kinds of curling irons! You know, to see which one gives a better, tighter, longer-lasting curl. Tell me it's a great idea! Because it is!"

Nora hardly knew how to begin. Nora's mother never curled her hair. Sarah never curled her hair. Nora never curled her hair. Hair curling wasn't something Alpers family women *did*.

"This will be awesome!" Emma went on. "I've been wanting to try different types of curling irons ever since, like, forever, and my mother won't buy any new ones for me, because she says the one I have is perfectly good, plus there's too much stuff all over the bathroom from me and my sister already. But if it's for *school,* she'd be fine with it, I know she would."

Nora had yet to find her voice.

"And don't worry, we'll make it super-scientific," Emma reassured Nora. "We'll take pictures of our curls at the start of the day, and then at every hour during the day, to see how they hold up under all different kinds of conditions."

"*Our* curls?" Nora finally made herself speak.

Emma's eyes fell on Nora's straw-straight hair.

"You'd look good in curls!" She hesitated. "Or maybe not. Look, we wouldn't both have to have curls. I'd be the one to try out all the different curling irons, and you'd be the one taking the pictures and making the graphs and things. You could find something to graph, right? You'd like that part, wouldn't you, Nora? So what do you think?"

I'm not going to do my *science-fair project on the best way to curl* your *hair!*

But Nora didn't want Emma to get all huffy again and start making more angry flower doodles on the cover of her science notebook.

Besides, it wasn't as if Emma's idea didn't have any scientific merit at all. It might be interesting to look at different kinds of curling irons and study how they worked, if different ones operated on different principles. Nora loved taking things apart to

68

figure out exactly how they performed their function. She had become the family expert on fixing the vacuum cleaner when it malfunctioned.

But curling irons? Curling irons were too un-Nora-ish. And would the judges pick a "Science of Curling Irons" project for the regional science fair?

Emma read Nora's answer from her pained silence.

"Well, what *are* we going to do?" Emma started coloring in the centers of her doodled flowers with sharp strokes of yellow marker. "We have to come up with *something*!"

Nora couldn't disagree with that.

And at least Emma's new idea had come from a real scientific question. At least it had begun the way science was supposed to, with something someone really, truly wanted to find out.

"Well," Nora said slowly, "maybe it could work. If we don't find anything better."

Emma beamed. "There couldn't be anything better, ever, ever, ever, because this idea is the best, best, best!"

Now Emma sounded a lot like Brody. And Nora was starting to feel a lot like Mason.

But at least they had come up with an idea,

however un-brilliant, un-amazing, un-fantastic, and un-fabuloso it might be.

Nora went to Mason's house after school that day with Mason and Brody. She always enjoyed going to Mason's house to taste his mother's homemade snacks and play with Mason's dog and hear all the funny negative things Mason said all the time about everything.

Now she had a new reason for wanting to go to Mason's house.

Mason had no newborn baby niece.

"Nora!" Mason's mother greeted her. "Tell us all about Nellie!"

Why was everyone else in the world so interested in babies?

"She cries a lot," Nora said.

"All babies do," Mrs. Dixon replied. "I bet she's darling!"

If you think it's darling to be bald.

Mason put four Fig Newtons on a plate and poured himself a glass of milk while his mother served mini spinach-and-feta-cheese quiches to

Nora and Brody. Mason had the world's shortest list of foods he was willing to eat. Nora took a first cautious bite of the quiche. It was delicious: the crust flaky, the filling warm and savory. Meals at Nora's house had gotten steadily worse since Nellie's arrival.

Mason's dog, Dog, rubbed himself against Nora's leg. Dog was actually as much Brody's dog as Mason's. He belonged to both boys equally, but he lived at Mason's house because Brody's dad was allergic to dogs and cats, to all pets except for Brody's goldfish, Albert.

"Did I cry a lot when I was a baby?" Mason asked, as Nora had the other day.

His mother hesitated before replying. "You weren't what I'd call an *easy* baby."

"Was I a *terrible* baby?"

He sounded almost eager to hear that he was.

"Well, I wouldn't say that any babies are *terrible*. I've never liked when people talk about *good* babies—'Oh, she's such a good baby, she's already sleeping through the night'—as if other babies are *bad*. Babies aren't good or bad. They're just babies."

Nora was pleased to hear Mason's mother

sounding like a fellow scientist. That was the kind of thing Nora was always having to tell other people. Her classmates would argue about whether dogs were good and cats were bad, or cats were good and dogs were bad, and she had to be the one to say that it didn't make any sense to say that dogs *or* cats were good *or* bad. They were just dogs and cats. Nora smiled at Mrs. Dixon.

"But if you *were* to say that a baby *was* terrible?" Mason prompted her.

His mother sighed. "Let's just say that there's a reason your father and I stopped at one."

"My mother told me I was the happiest baby anybody had ever seen," Brody put in after swallowing his fifth mini quiche. "One time, I was out in the backyard playing in my sandbox, and I was laughing so much the neighbors came over to find out what was so funny."

"And?" Mason asked. "What *was* so funny?"

"Nothing! I was laughing because I was so happy."

Nora had felt glad the other day to learn that she had been filled with scientific curiosity from the very start. But hearing about Mason's baby

WORLD'S HAPPIEST ·B·A·B·Y·

crankiness and Brody's baby joyfulness gave her a strange feeling inside. Did you pop out in the world already being the person you were going to be?

As a scientist, Nora knew about genes: the biological markers that determined whether you had straight dark hair like hers or curly blond hair like Emma's—well, assuming that Emma's hair was curly even without her curling iron. Genes determined whether you were a girl or a boy. But did they also decide whether you would be crabby or cheerful, would be talented at science or art, would like learning about fashion or ants?

"So," Nora said, to chase the strange feeling away, "what are you guys doing for your science-fair project?"

"It's great!" Brody said just as Mason said, "It's dumb."

Nora and Mrs. Dixon grinned at each other.

"You know how everybody says that if you drop a piece of toast on the floor, it always falls butter-side down?" Brody asked her.

Nora had never heard anybody say that, but she nodded anyway. She wasn't sure why anyone would even care which side buttered toast fell on in the first place.

"People say that," Mason's mother explained, "because it seems so often that you have to go get a sponge to wipe the butter off the carpet."

"Oh," Nora said. She still couldn't believe that enough people dropped buttered slices of toast onto carpets to generate any famous saying about it.

"Our project"—Brody paused to beat out a drum-roll on the kitchen table—"is to find out, once and for all, if that's true."

It wasn't a *great* project, in Nora's opinion, but it wasn't a dumb project, either. It was always worthwhile to try to find out if things that "everybody" said were true or false.

"We're going to butter lots and lots of pieces of toast," Brody continued, "and drop them lots and lots of times, and count how many times they fall butter-side up and how many times they fall butter-side down."

"Where exactly are you planning on doing these experiments?" Mrs. Dixon asked.

"Not on the carpet," Brody assured her. "On the floor. If any butter gets on the floor, Dog can lick it up."

"Now, boys—" Mrs. Dixon said.

"Coach Joe said we didn't have to do the *whole* project at school," Brody told her, as if that had been her worry. "We can do some of it at home, so long as we do it without any parental assistance. Though I guess if we do the experiments ourselves, but our parents mop the floor off afterward, that much parental help would be okay."

"I'm sure Coach Joe would want you boys to do your own mopping," Mason's mother said. "And *I'd* expect you to do your own mopping. But here and now, I'm decreeing that no buttered toast is going to be dropped onto any floor in anybody's house. There's no reason you can't drop your toast outside."

"I bet it doesn't always fall butter-side down," Brody predicted.

"I bet it does," Mason said.

"What about you, Nora?" Mrs. Dixon asked. "What's your project going to be this time? I still remember what a terrific project you had last year on water quality in the creek. I told Mason's father that it should be published in a scientific journal."

The compliment gave Nora a pang. She had tried to publish an article in a scientific journal once, and it had gotten rejected. And no scientific journal was going to want to publish an article about curling irons!

"I don't know yet," Nora said, unable to come out with the truth.

"I'm sure you'll come up with something splendid," Mrs. Dixon told her.

Nora forced a smile. It was all too likely the curling-iron idea was going to fall butter-side down.

When a baby starts out life as a fertilized egg, it is smaller than a grain of sand. But it already has a full set of 46 chromosomes, all the genetic material it is ever going to have, the whole blueprint for deciding hair color, eye color, height, and maybe even personality?

In the team huddle on Thursday, Coach Joe invited people to share some of their diary entries from the Oregon Trail.

Brody's hand was first up, of course.

Bill Breeden here, with my faithful dog, Pup. I don't have no family, except for Pup, but Pup is all I need. I have him, and he has me. I hope we'll always have each other.

Brody's voice wobbled. Nora knew he was remembering that Bill Breeden was going to die of a fever in Wyoming. What would happen to Pup then?

Maybe Amy's rattlesnake-braving pioneer, Sally Hamilton, could adopt him. Sally probably loved pets as much as Amy did.

Brody could never stay sad for long, however. His happy smile returned as he kept on reading.

My faithful horse, Albert, is hitched up to go.

Brody had named Bill's horse after his own goldfish, Albert.

Maybe Amy's Sally would have to adopt Albert, too.

Or Nora's Martha could. Martha definitely loved all kinds of animals. At least, she loved writing journal entries about all kinds of animals. That was all Martha had written about in the three journal entries Nora had completed so far: one on crows, one on wolves, and one on porcupines. She had yet to make a single mention of Tom Talbot or her two older children. The only thing she ever said about her baby was to end some entries, "Baby's crying! Got to go!"

Brody kept on reading.

My wagon is filled with all the stuff I'll need on the trail. Blankets, dried meat, lots of potatoes, flour for pancakes, and syrup to pour on my pancakes. I will be fine, whatever happens, so long as I have plenty of pancakes.

Pup, Albert, and I are ready for an adventure. Some folks say there will be hardships on the trail. Pup, Albert, and I don't mind. All three of us like adventures. We're happy when we go to new places and meet new people and see new things. And eat new pancakes!

The head of our wagon train, Jake Smith, says he has a bad feeling about the trip. But he has a bad feeling about a lot of things. Not me. I think it's going to be great!

I really do!

Coach Joe grinned when Brody finished. It was hard not to grin when Brody's own grin was so infectious.

"Bill What's-His-Name isn't going to think everything's so great when he croaks in Wyoming," Dunk said.

Brody shrugged. "Maybe I won't die." He looked over at Coach Joe. "Do I *have* to die?"

Nora waited to hear what Coach Joe would say. Did Martha Talbot *have* to be married to Tom Talbot?

"I do want each of you to stick true with what's written on your fate card," Coach Joe said. "That's the assignment."

"Well, Wyoming is a long ways away," Brody told Dunk. "I might as well be happy *now*, right?"

"That's the spirit, Brody!" Coach Joe said.

Two other kids read: Tamara, who was sick with a horrible disease called dysentery, and a boy named Ned, whose pioneer apparently liked writing very short and very boring diary entries.

"We'll hear from more of you next time," Coach Joe told the class. "And we're going to hear from *all* of you at the end of next week when we make a class documentary about your experiences on the trail. A *documentary* is a nonfiction film that *documents*—reports—information about some important thing that happened, usually showing real people talking about real events. For our class documentary, the real people will be all of you, and the real events will be things that happened to you on the Oregon Trail."

"We're going to be in a movie?" Emma squealed, fluffing her curls as if filming were about to begin any minute. Emma was probably already planning out what she would wear to the Academy Awards.

"Well, not a Hollywood movie," Coach Joe said. "More of a video, just for our class. A few of our parent helpers will assist us in filming it. It'll be pretty cool, I think, to have an instant replay of our time together on the Oregon Trail."

"Do we dress up for it?" Emma asked.

Mason groaned. Mason hated dressing up, even on Halloween.

"Definitely! Do what you can to find yourself some pioneer duds, but don't stress too much if you can't come up with anything. Bring in any props you can think of, too. A sack of pancake flour, Brody? Anything to add some authenticity to our film."

Emma whispered to Nora, "Bring Nellie!"

Nora smiled weakly.

She had yet to ask Sarah about the Saturday Nellie-viewing party, even though Saturday was now two days away. Sarah was so close to tears all the time now, from lack of sleep and problems getting Nellie to nurse, that Nora hadn't dared to mention it.

And now she was supposed to ask if Nellie could be a prop for the class Oregon Trail documentary?

Why was it okay to use Nellie as a prop in a movie but not to do a few little experiments with her for the science fair?

Nora would never understand other people.

Especially Emma.

After school, Nora and Amy rode with Amy's mother to the Plainfield Animal Shelter. No, Amy wasn't looking for a new pet to adopt. Instead, now that the YMCA basketball season was over, the girls had signed up to volunteer once a week taking care of the shelter animals, while Amy's brother, Sheridan, was off at gymnastics.

In the car, Nora hardly listened as Amy explained the science-fair idea she and Anthony had come up with: testing which colors birds liked best. They were going to put out different colors of birdseed—from the same bag, but dyed in all the hues of the rainbow—and see which one Amy's two parakeets ate first.

You have to ask Sarah about the party! Nora kept reciting to herself over and over again. *You have to ask Sarah about the party!*

"What about you and Emma?" Amy asked. "You're so scientific, and, well, Emma's not, and so I'm wondering what kind of idea you'll come up with."

Nora was going to have to tell Amy their dopey

curling-iron idea sometime. It might as well be now.

"We're going to . . ." Nora swallowed hard, and then the rest of the words came out in a rush. "We're going to test different kinds of curling irons to see which one makes the best and tightest curl and why. We haven't started doing the actual experiments yet, because Emma's parents have to go buy the curling irons, but they're going to get them this weekend, and then we can start curling Emma's hair and discover . . . whatever we discover."

She couldn't bear to look at Amy's face. But when she did, Amy was wreathed in smiles and tugged happily on the end of her braid, tied with pink ribbons today to match her new pink polka-dot sweater.

"That's super cool, Nora, it is! You can send the results to that magazine my dad gets that publishes articles on which is the best toaster, and which is the best computer tablet, and which is the best *everything*. Maybe they'd do a story about you and Emma, and you'll be famous."

"You really think it's not dumb?" Nora asked.

"Definitely not!" Amy promised her. "Only . . ."

"Only what?"

"You're not going to curl *your* hair, are you?"

Nora laughed. "Of course not! Emma will be the one with the curls, and I'll be the one analyzing the results."

Amy looked relieved. "I mean, you'd look good in curls, I'm sure you would. But you wouldn't look like *you*. You wouldn't look like Nora."

Nora couldn't disagree with that.

A newborn baby's heart beats between 130 and 160 times per minute, about twice as fast as a normal adult's. I wonder why that is. Maybe their hearts need to beat faster because they are growing and changing so much?

At the shelter, the man at the front desk, whose name tag read BRAD, welcomed them and explained a bunch of rules they had to follow. He pointed out the loop trail behind the building, where they would be taking pairs of dogs out on short exercise walks.

The girls waited, and then Brad returned with a Great Dane on one leash and a small corgi mix on the other.

"Here's Duke for you." He handed the Great Dane's leash to Nora. "And Bubbles for *you*." He handed the other leash to Amy. An adult was required to be present at all times with any volunteers under age fifteen, so Mrs. Talia walked behind the girls as they headed out to the trail. But she let them handle the dogs on their own.

Nora tried to give her full attention to Duke, but all she could think about was the baby-viewing party, which was now less than forty-eight hours away.

"Earth to Nora," Amy said. "I told you three adorable things Bubbles did, and I don't think you heard a single word I said."

Nora couldn't deny it. She could feel her face settling into a worried frown.

"What's wrong?" Amy asked. "I mean, you have a huge, wonderful dog on a leash, *and* a way-cool science-fair idea, *and* you get to be an aunt, *and* we all get to meet Nellie on Saturday!"

Nora tried to smile. The dog walking was a good thing, and Amy had given the curling-iron project two thumbs up, but it wasn't going to be even a tiny bit fun being an aunt when Sarah found out about the baby-viewing party.

Maybe Amy would find a way to be as positive about the baby-viewing party as she had been about the curling irons.

"I haven't told Sarah about the Nellie party yet," Nora confessed. "She seems so stressed about everything right now. I didn't want to make her even more stressed. But if I don't tell her, and Emma and everybody show up on Saturday, then she's going to be super-duper-mega-crazy stressed, and it'll be all my fault."

"Oh," Amy said.

Nora had hoped Amy would have something more helpful to offer than that.

"Okay," Amy said, rising to the occasion. "As soon as we get home today, *just tell her.* Things like this are always better than you think they're going to be. Like when I found Woofer? He was a stray, and I hid him in the backyard shed, and for three whole days I died inside every single minute, terrified to tell my parents about him for fear they'd say I couldn't keep him and we'd have to take him right here, to the animal shelter. But then I finally did tell them, and they said no problem, it was fine to keep him, and I felt soooo much better."

"But what if they hadn't said that? What if they had said the thing you were afraid they'd say?"

"But they didn't," Amy pointed out.

"But *Sarah* might. She might tell me that I can't have the party, and then I'd have to tell Emma, and, well, you know how Emma is."

"Oh" was all that Amy could think of to say.

Neither Duke nor Bubbles had anything to offer, either. And after walking border collie Max and huge mutt Mister T., while Amy walked toy poodle Toby and terrier Susie Q., Nora was still as stuck as ever.

The first thing Nora noticed when she entered the living room was how completely different her house looked now from how it had looked one short week ago.

The smaller the human being, the greater the volume of stuff that went along with it.

A baby bouncer stood next to a baby car seat, which stood next to a baby stroller, which stood next to a baby windup swing.

To Nora's great relief, no actual baby was in any of those baby containers right now. The actual baby was probably upstairs sleeping in her baby bassinet.

Piles of laundry covered the couch. Not baby laundry, just everybody's laundry that nobody had gotten around to folding and putting away because everyone was so busy fussing over Nellie. When Nora headed into the kitchen, she saw dirty dishes covering every available surface for the same reason. Nora's parents had someone come every other week to clean the house, but this wasn't cleaning week. And Julie, the cleaner, would probably have taken one look at the Alperses' house right now and quit on the spot.

Somebody had to do something. Nora knew she was that somebody.

She set to work folding laundry, rinsing dishes, and loading the dishwasher, as well as picking up stuffed animals—how many stuffed animals did a week-old baby really need?—and putting them in the baby toy basket that stood next to the bouncer, car seat, stroller, and swing.

Pleased with her progress, she was wiping down the sticky kitchen counters when Sarah appeared in the doorway, still in her bathrobe, her hair tangled and matted, clearly in need of washing.

"Wow," Sarah said, staring at the transformed kitchen with bewilderment. "What got into *you*?"

Nora shrugged. "I figured I'd help clean up a bit." Now might be a good time to mention the party. "You know, in case some people dropped by or something."

Already pale, Sarah turned even paler.

"If any people even *thought* of dropping by, I'd . . ." The sentence was evidently too terrible for Sarah to finish. "I haven't washed my hair in a *week*! I haven't had a shower since . . . *Monday*? I've had maybe ten hours of sleep total since Nellie was *born*!"

So would it be okay if five of my friends came over for a little party the day after tomorrow?

No. She couldn't follow Amy's advice. She just couldn't. Not now. Not yet. Not ever.

Nora finished wiping the counters and rinsed out the sponge. Maybe Sarah would feel better now that the kitchen was clean. Maybe between today and Saturday, she'd have a chance to wash her hair and get some sleep.

Or maybe not.

"Well, at least the kitchen looks better," Nora said brightly. "That's something, right?"

For an answer came Nellie's wake-up wail and Sarah's weary sigh.

During science time on Friday, Nora and Emma sat side by side at one of the classroom computers, trying to figure out which curling irons Emma's parents should buy for her that weekend. There were so many different kinds! There was something called a curling iron and something else called a curling wand. They had different heat settings—as many as thirty for some of the higher-priced irons. There were different-sized "barrels" to wrap your hair around. Some were made of metal, some of ceramic. They had different voltages.

See? Nora wanted to say to Emma. *They use volts!*

"Oh, and there's different stuff to use with them, too," Emma added happily. "There's thermal product, and styling spray, and volumizing mousse, and—"

Nora's head was reeling. It was clear that there were enough different variables here for twenty science-fair projects.

"Are you sure your parents are going to want to spend all this money on these things?" she interrupted. "Some of these curling irons cost over a hundred dollars."

"Nora," Emma reminded her, "this is for *science*. It's worth spending money for the sake of *science*, don't you agree?"

As if Nora would disagree!

From across the room, Nora could hear Brody's

raised voice. "And our dog, Dog? It turns out he *loves* pieces of buttered toast lying on the ground, butter-side up *or* butter-side down! It's his new favorite food!"

Nora could see Sheng busily working away on an experiment for converting potential energy to kinetic energy, while Dunk was busily working away on nothing. Sheng was doing everything, but Dunk would get the same grade and half the credit. It was so unfair. Nora wished Coach Joe would say something, but he was busy helping Amy and Anthony figure out how to graph their birdseed-color results.

"So . . . ," Emma said, once they had finally picked their four top-choice curling irons for her parents to buy. "About the party tomorrow?"

We can't have it! Because we need to spend the whole weekend testing these curling irons for the science fair!

Emma went on. "I was thinking it might be too much for you and your sister right now."

Well, that, too.

"You shouldn't have to do all that party planning, with a new baby and all," Emma went on.

Nora felt weak with relief. Lots of time to test out curling irons! No stress with Sarah! Yes, yes, yes!

"So," Emma said, "I'm volunteering to help."

"Help?" Nora asked in a strangled voice.

"Like, with the decorations. And the food."

Nora opened her mouth. No sound came out. But she had to make herself say something!

She finally found her voice. "I think—given everything—that we should—"

"Keep it simple," Emma finished her sentence. "Totally! Simple is great! So just some pink balloons, especially on the mailbox so that everyone can find your house. And a pink tablecloth for the table. I bet you don't even have a pink tablecloth. Am I right?"

Emma took Nora's stunned silence for an affirmative reply.

"I knew it!" Emma said. "Well, *I* have a pink tablecloth, so you don't have to worry about that. And my mom said she'd take me shopping after school today to get some paper plates, cups, and napkins that say IT'S A GIRL! There's nothing simpler than paper plates. I know what you're going to say, that they're not good for the environment, but this one time I think it's okay."

Nora watched as Emma produced a small flower-shaped notepad from her desk and started a shopping list: balloons, plates, cups, napkins.

"Now, food," Emma said. "How are you set for party food? That can be simple, too. Punch with sherbet floating on top. I love sherbet punch! And cookies—pink-frosted. And some fruit to make it healthy. Wait—fruit skewers! I helped my mom make them for her bridge club. You get these little wooden sticks, and you put on one strawberry, one chunk of pineapple, one chunk of banana, and one big green grape. That's all! Easy-peasy!"

"Emma—" Nora said, but it was impossible to interrupt Emma in full party-planning mode. "Emma—"

"Look, *I'll* make the skewers. Don't worry! You and your sister won't have to do a thing for the skewers."

To the list, Emma added strawberries, pine-apple, bananas, grapes, skewers.

"So all you and Sarah have to take care of is the cookies and the punch. You do know how to make punch, don't you? Just buy, say, four cans of frozen punch, and mix it with some club soda so it's fizzy, and then dump some raspberry sherbet on top. Ta-da! I told you we could keep this simple and easy."

"*Emma.*"

"And don't feel you have to *bake* cookies," Emma went on. "Everyone will understand if they're store-bought. I could even get the cookies when I get the other stuff. You can pay me back for everything afterward. Really. It's okay."

To the list, Emma added: cookies.

"So the only thing left—"

Besides getting Sarah ever to speak to Nora again.

"—is . . . party favors!"

"I don't think we need party favors," Nora said faintly.

Now it was Emma's turn to stare at Nora.

"Are you kidding? Party favors are the best part! Except for seeing Nellie, of course. That's the *best* best part. I'm going to make the party favors, too. I already have the perfect idea. Wait till you see them, Nora. You're going to think they're the most adorable thing ever. I promise!"

"Huddle!" Coach Joe called to the class.

"With the party tomorrow, and playing with—I mean, experimenting with—the curling irons on Sunday, this is going to be a great weekend!" Emma said happily.

More likely, it would be the worst weekend of Nora's life.

A baby triples its birth weight by the end of the first year. If we did that every year, we'd weigh almost 2,000 pounds by the time we were 5 years old!

Nora sat in her bedroom that evening talking to her ants.

She wasn't in the habit of talking to them. Her ants didn't know or care that they belonged to a human girl named Nora Alpers who right now was in the worst trouble of her life. Nora had studied ants long enough to understand that they had problems of their own to worry about: collapsed tunnels, variable soil conditions. Not that ants *worried* about such things. Their brains were too small for worry. Worrying wasn't what ants *did*.

Lucky ants!

"Here are my options," Nora said aloud to her ants, even though she knew they weren't listening. Ants communicated mostly through chemical secretions rather than through spoken speech.

"Option number one: I do what Amy said and tell Sarah tonight. And then she'll freak out, and Mom and Dad will make me call Emma and cancel the party, and Emma's already bought the balloons and the skewers and the fruit for the skewers and the pink-frosted cookies, and *she'll* freak out and hate me forever, and Bethy, Tamara, and Elise will hate me forever, too, though probably not as much as Emma will hate me. And Emma will never speak to me again, and our curling-iron project will be the worst one in the history of the school."

Nora paused. One of her ants was so motionless that it appeared to be listening through the glass wall of the ant farm.

But maybe it was asleep.

Or maybe it was dead.

Sometimes it was hard to tell with ants.

"Option number two: I *don't* tell Sarah, and everybody will just show up at party time with the balloons and the food and all the other stuff, and Sarah will freak out in front of Emma, and they'll *both* hate me forever."

Nora reflected on that scenario.

"No, Sarah wouldn't do that. She'd be polite to Emma, so *Emma* won't hate me forever, but *Sarah* will. So I'll keep my science-fair partner, but lose my only sister."

Nora reached into her ant farm and poked the listening/sleeping/dead ant with a little stick. It scurried away.

"Option number three . . . ," Nora said.

Please let there be an option number three!

"Option number three . . . ," she repeated, thinking as hard as she could as the ant rejoined its fellow ants down the closest tunnel.

"Okay. Option number three is that I clean the house all morning so it basically looks okay. I tell Sarah an hour before the party so that she has time to take a shower while I take care of Nellie."

Nora gulped at that part. She could vacuum a living room and tidy a kitchen. She didn't think she could take care of a baby. She had passed up so many opportunities to hold Nellie that Sarah and her parents had stopped even asking.

Nora corrected the plan. "I'll tell Sarah an hour before so she can have a shower and get changed while *Mom and Dad* take care of Nellie. And I'll make sure she knows how hard I tried to make the party not happen."

Well, she *would* have tried if she had even known how to try.

"What do you think?" Nora asked her ants.

The ants made no reply. Nora hadn't expected any. And she didn't need their response.

Option number three wasn't a terrific option, by any means, but at this point, it was all she had.

"No. *No.* NO."

With each *no,* Sarah's voice rose higher.

"They won't stay very long. I promise." Nora cast a nervous eye on the kitchen clock. It was an hour till party time, but Emma had said she'd come early to help. Nora wasn't sure how early Emma's "early" was going to be.

"Who isn't going to stay very long?" her mother

asked, coming into the kitchen, still in her pajamas like her older daughter.

"Emma," Nora said. "Well, Emma and Bethy. Well, Tamara, too. And Elise and Amy."

"They're all coming *here*?" Her mother sounded as panicked as Sarah looked. "Is this for a group project at school? Surely there has to be someone else's house you can meet at, a house that doesn't have a baby who's barely a week old in it!"

"No," Nora said. "It's not a school thing. Nellie is the *reason* they're coming. She's the whole *point* of the party."

"Of the *party*?" Nora's sister and mother shrieked at the same time.

"It's a party to see Nellie," Nora tried to explain. If only they wouldn't both stare at her that way!

She tried again. "It wasn't my idea. The idea all came from Emma."

Truer words had never been spoken.

"The house looks okay," Nora pointed out. "I cleaned *all morning*." She gestured toward the swept floor, the gleaming counters. "And Emma's doing most of the work. She's the one bringing the cookies, and the fruit skewers, and the balloons, and the pink tablecloth. All we have to do is make the sherbet punch."

At the words *sherbet punch,* Sarah's face crumpled and she buried her head in her hands.

"Nora, what were you thinking?" her mother demanded. "This isn't like you!"

It was terrible to hear the disappointment in her mother's voice. Her mother was right. This *wasn't* like her. It also wasn't like her to be curling Emma's hair for the science fair. Or to be on the Oregon Trail married to Dunk! Lately nothing in Nora's life was the way it was supposed to be, except for her ants.

The doorbell rang.

With one last glare at Nora, Sarah turned and fled. But Nora's mother held her ground, apparently undaunted by the thought of having a guest see her wearing pajamas in the afternoon. Actually she was wearing her husband's too-large pajamas, as her own were in the dryer.

Slowly, Nora made herself go to the front door and open it a crack.

There stood Emma and Bethy. Emma held a large shopping bag in one hand and balanced a tray loaded with fruit skewers in the other. Bethy carried a second large shopping bag, as well as an enormous bunch of pink balloons that looked ready to carry her off in the stiff March breeze.

"We're here!" Emma announced. "Bethy came early, too, because there was too much for one person to carry."

Emma's mother waved from the car and drove away.

There was no turning back now.

"Come in," Nora said.

What else could she say? If her mother was really set on canceling the party, let her be the one to do it.

Emma's eyes darted around the crowded living room. "Where is she? Where's Nellie? Oh, Bethy, look! There's her stroller!"

"And her car seat!"

"And her little bouncy thingie!"

"And her swing!"

"She's asleep," Nora said in a low voice, hoping Nellie could sleep with all of Emma and Bethy's squealing.

Nora's mother appeared in the doorway that led from the living room into the kitchen.

"Girls, I don't think—"

"We're here to set up!" Emma proclaimed, not seeming to notice either Nora's mother's pj's or her frown. "Bethy's going to tie a few of the balloons onto the mailbox. Nothing says party-party-party like balloons on the mailbox, don't you think? Let's tie one on her swing, too, and one on the stroller— on all of her super-adorable things. Bethy said we got too many balloons, but I don't think you can *have* too many balloons, do you?"

Nora's mother opened her mouth and shut it again.

That could be a science-fair question right there: How could one ten-year-old girl transform a world-famous expert on the rings of Saturn into a gaping goldfish?

"Where should we put the food?" Emma asked. "In the kitchen? Nora, wait till you see the cookies. They're not just pink-frosted cookies; they're pink-frosted *tulip* cookies! And we'll need a spot to put the presents."

"The kitchen is fine," Nora's mother managed to say.

"Nora, close your eyes," Emma commanded. "Mrs. Alpers, you close your eyes, too."

Nora obeyed. She had no idea if her mother had done the same. She could hear Emma fumbling about in one of the shopping bags.

"Okay. You can open them now!"

Emma handed Nora and her mother each a tiny plastic baby bottle, capped with a pink nipple and tied with a pink bow. The bottle was filled with brown powder topped with little white balls.

"The party favors!" Emma beamed. "The brown stuff is hot-chocolate mix. You should have *seen* how long it took to strain it to get out all the marshmallows so I could put them on the top of each one. Don't you think they look better with the mini-marshmallows on top?"

Her face alight with excitement, Emma led the way into the kitchen, with Bethy following, still clutching the enormous bunch of pink balloons straining upward toward the ceiling.

Nora's mother gave Nora a quick, forgiving hug.

"I understand now," she apologized. "I understand everything."

Newborn babies breathe about 40 times a minute. An adult breathes between 12 and 20 times a minute. Maybe this is connected with the fact that a baby's heart beats more often than an adult's? When I have to host a baby-viewing party, I think I breathe faster and have a faster heart rate. Something to check.

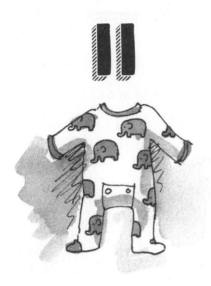

When Sarah made her grand entrance to the party an hour later, dressed, hair washed and combed, and carrying a wide-awake, non-crying Nellie, the rapture of the party guests knew no bounds.

"Nellie!" five girls squealed at once, including Amy.

At the sudden noise, Nellie's small face scrunched itself into pre-crying mode.

"Shush!" Emma instructed the others in a loud whisper. "Use indoor voices!"

Fortunately, Nellie decided not to cry. There was no way she could know that the pink tablecloth, pink balloons, and spread of party food were in her honor. But she did seem to be looking around the room with bright eyes, taking it all in.

"Is it okay if we come closer?" Tamara asked.

Sarah nodded.

"One at a time!" Emma told them, for all the world as if this were *her* house and Nellie were *her* niece. But Nora was glad to have someone else taking charge. She herself had no idea what people were supposed to do at a baby-admiration party.

Emma had been nice about the lack of sherbet punch, too. "It's okay," she had told Nora. "Once they see Nellie, they won't care about anything else!" Then Nora had worried that Sarah might refuse to appear with Nellie. What kind of baby-admiration party would that be, with no sherbet punch *and* no baby? Or Nellie might cry the whole time. But here was Sarah, and here was Nellie, and no one was crying. Yet.

The girls filed past Nellie.

"Look at her fingers!"

"They're so itty-bitty!"

"I love her booties!"

"That is the cutest dress ever!"

"Her eyes are so blue!"

"They probably won't stay blue," Sarah said. "Most Caucasian—white—babies are born with blue eyes, but only a fifth of them have blue eyes later on."

Now, that was another fascinating fact for her notebook, Nora thought. Why would that be? What could cause infant eyes to change color?

She was oddly relieved to find out that babies could change their eye color. If even eye color wasn't fixed at birth, maybe other things about babies could change, too, like personality. Maybe Brody could have grown up to be grumpy, and Mason could have grown up to be cheerful.

Despite Emma's command, all the girls, Emma included, were now crowded around Nellie, who was still snuggled safe in Sarah's arms. Only Nora stood apart. She could see Nellie anytime she wanted. Plus lots of times she *didn't* want.

"Do you think . . . ?" Amy asked then.

"You don't suppose . . . ?" Elise tried to help her out.

"Would it be all right?" Tamara asked.

"If we were really careful?" Bethy put in.

"Could we *hold* her?" Emma finished.

Sarah hesitated. But then she smiled. "Nobody has a cold, right? Not even a sniffle?"

Everyone shook her head.

"Okay. Go wash your hands with plenty of soap and hot water. I'll sit on the couch in the family room, and you can come sit next to me and take turns holding her."

Great was the excitement as the girls hurried to the kitchen and took turns squirting their hands with soap and scrubbing them under hot water. Nora filed into the kitchen with them but held back to let the others have the first turn at the sink. She didn't really need a turn, as the last thing she planned on doing was holding Nellie in front of a large, fascinated audience. But as the others raced back to the room, Nora, not to be left out, gave her hands a quick dousing.

She returned to the family room just as Sarah was finishing with giving her baby-holding instructions. It was almost comical, in Nora's opinion, how much of a fuss Sarah was making about simply holding a baby. Human beings had held human infants ever since humankind had existed. And before that, grown-up apes had held baby apes without washing their hands with hot soapy water and memorizing an instruction manual.

"All right, girls," Sarah said. "Who wants to go first?"

All of a sudden, the girls turned shy, as if no one, not even Emma, felt she merited the honor of being the very first one to hold Nellie.

"Nora, you're her aunt," Emma said. "You can show us how."

"I don't think . . ." Nora had planned to say that she didn't think people needed an official baby-holding demonstration. And they certainly didn't need one from someone who had never yet held a baby herself.

But with five pairs of expectant eyes upon her, Nora somehow found herself sitting on the couch next to Sarah, trying to look more confident than she felt, which meant trying to look confident at all.

Sarah handed Nora the baby. As Nora awkwardly attempted to settle Nellie on her lap, the baby's surprisingly large head lurched to one side.

"Nora!" Sarah cried out. "Weren't you listening? You have to support her head! Her neck muscles aren't strong enough yet! If you don't support her neck, it can break!"

At this, Nellie began to cry. Surely her neck wasn't already broken! Surely she had just been awakened by Sarah's near shriek.

Sarah scooped a wailing Nellie back into her own arms and cradled her close as Nora jumped up from the couch and stood as far away as possible from Nellie on the other side of the room.

The other girls, except for Amy, stared at Nora with apparent disapproval in their eyes, as if she had almost broken Nellie's neck on purpose instead of merely being a clumsy young aunt who had happened to be out of the room at the wrong time.

There was a pained silence, except for Nellie's whimpers. No one else seemed to want to be the next one to run the risk of breaking Nellie.

Some party this was turning out to be!

Finally Emma plopped herself down in Nora's abandoned spot. Unlike Nora, Emma made sure to place a careful hand on the back of Nellie's neck. Unlike Nora, Emma lit up with pleasure as Nellie grasped her pinkie finger.

"She likes me!" Emma said. "Look! She's holding on to my finger! Yes, Nellie-Bellie, this is your auntie Emma, yes, it is!"

"Ohhh!" the girls chorused. "Awww!"

In turn, Nellie was held, neck properly supported,

by Auntie Bethy, Auntie Elise, Auntie Tamara, and Auntie Amy.

"Maybe I won't be a veterinarian," Amy announced as she let Sarah reclaim Nellie. "Maybe I'll be a pediatrician!"

The only one who had failed at being an aunt was the only one who was Nellie's real aunt: Aunt Nora.

"Presents?" Sarah asked, once the cookies and fruit skewers had been devoured. No one had complained at all about the pitcher of ice water Nora's mother had brought out.

"See?" Emma whispered to Nora. "I told you nobody would mind about the sherbet punch."

Sarah stared in puzzlement at the first of the five beautifully wrapped boxes Emma was holding out to her.

"Oh, girls, you didn't need to bring us anything," Nora's mother said. "The balloons, the cookies, the lovely fruit—it's already too much."

"We wanted to," Emma said. "Truly we did. We all think Nora is sooooo lucky."

Nora had never in her life felt less lucky. Why did

babies have to be so complicated! So fragile and noisy and unpredictable! So utterly unlike ants.

Sarah set Nellie in her little bouncer and sat down in the rocking chair beside her. One by one, she opened the presents.

A little sleeper patterned with pink elephants.

A soft pink blanket with a pink giraffe embroidered on it.

A tiny pink sweater covered with yellow flowers with pink centers.

A stuffed pink unicorn.

A baby-sized T-shirt that said PINK PRINCESS.

Sarah exclaimed over all of them as Nora's mother wrote down each gift and the name of its giver so that Sarah could send thank-you notes.

Presumably to be written on pink note cards.

Still stinging from her all-too-public aunt failure, Nora felt herself becoming more and more irritated. Did every single thing Nellie owned have to be pink? What was wrong with a gray elephant, the color elephants were in nature? What was wrong with a brown-and-tan giraffe, the colors giraffes were in nature? Surely Amy, who had given the giraffe blanket, knew better than that. And a *unicorn*? A totally imaginary creature that didn't exist in nature at all? And why assume that every girl wanted to be a princess, let alone a pink princess?

Nora certainly didn't.

Except for Emma, who stayed to help clean up, the other girls were collected by their parents at three-thirty.

Nellie had finally started wailing.

"Because she doesn't want her party to be over," Emma explained.

Nora wished the party had never begun.

Sarah had carried Nellie upstairs to nurse. Nora's mother had disappeared into her home office. Her father, who was at the university, had missed the whole thing, which Nora knew he wouldn't mind a bit.

Emma covered the leftover fruit skewers with plastic wrap and put them in Nora's fridge. She was certainly comfortable in somebody else's kitchen.

"Well, *that* was a perfect party," Emma said, with a happy sigh.

Emma's definition of *perfect* couldn't have been more different from Nora's.

"So," Nora said, eager to change the subject, "what time should I come over tomorrow?"

"Tomorrow?" Emma asked, as if she had no idea what Nora was talking about.

"The science fair? The curling irons? Temperature settings, barrel size, ceramic versus metal?"

A shadow passed over Emma's previously smiling face. The girl who had been so capable in organizing a baby party, cleaning up after a baby party, and holding the baby herself during the baby party now looked strangely ill at ease.

"Nora, there's, well, there's a teensy problem."

"What kind of problem?"

"It's my parents. They're being totally ridiculous. I mean, I told them and told them and told them about how we need the curling irons for the science fair, and we need them this weekend, but my dad rolled his eyes and said, 'Three hundred dollars? You've got to be kidding,' and my mom said, 'What about that science-fair project where you make a volcano out of vinegar and baking soda?'"

Nora stared at Emma, unable to believe what she was hearing.

"I'm sorry, I really am," Emma said. "But they

said no to the curling irons, and I couldn't talk them into it, and you know how good I am at talking people into things."

Nora knew all too well that Emma had talked her into another complete disaster.

Sarah was right. Most Caucasian babies have grayish blue eyes, and the color often changes by the fifth or sixth month. Most babies of other races have brown eyes, and the color doesn't change.

12

"So exactly when were you going to get around to telling me?" Nora asked in as icy a tone as she could manage, given the rage that was boiling up in her.

"I didn't want to spoil the party," Emma said in a small voice.

"I didn't want to *have* the party," Nora burst out. "But you came barging in with pink everything, and Sarah's still mad at me about it, I know she is." Sarah wouldn't have yelled at Nora in front of everyone if she hadn't already been angry about having the party sprung on her with minutes to spare. "And *you're* the one who wanted me to do *my* science-fair project on the best way to curl *your* hair, and now it's ruined, and the science fair is less than a week away, and we have nothing, nothing at all, except a house full of . . . pinkness. I. Hate. Pink!"

Even as she said it, she realized what an un-Nora-like thing it was to say. How could you *hate* a *color*? It made no sense to have such a strong emotional reaction to a certain wavelength of light! But it was all too much, this whole terrible day.

"We'll think of something else," Emma said soothingly. "And the party was wonderful. And Nellie looks adorable in pink, she really does."

It was easier for Nora to focus her anger on the color pink rather than on her failure as an aunt or her smashed-to-smithereens science-fair dreams. "Why does everyone have to give baby girls pink things?" Nora demanded. "Who decided that girls have to have everything pink, and boys have to have everything blue?"

"I don't know," Emma said, calmly wiping up

cookie crumbs from the dining room table as if her bombshell announcement hadn't just destroyed Nora's life. "I don't think anybody *decided* that. Pink just looks girlish, and blue looks boyish. I feel pretty when I wear pink. And other people look at me different when I dress up like a girl."

"But that's dumb!" Nora protested. "Why should *clothes* make a person feel different? Why should *clothes* make other people react that way?"

"They just do."

"Clothes don't make *me* feel different when I wear them," Nora said. "Unless they're really uncomfortable or something. And *I* don't treat other people differently because of the clothes they wear."

"Well," Emma said. It was obvious she was trying to be tactful in what she said next. "You're different from most people, Nora. You are. And I bet you *would* feel different if you were wearing pink. Do you ever wear pink?"

"No," Nora admitted. She had never put her thoughts about clothing in general and pink clothing in particular to a scientific test.

"I have an idea," Emma said slowly. "You're the

one who likes experiments. So for all next week, you should wear something pink every day."

"I don't *have* anything pink."

"You can borrow one of my pink sweaters. Like this one."

Emma pulled her pink sweater out of her bag, and handed it to Nora.

"Wear a different pink sweater every single day; I have tons I can loan you. And see how you feel and how other people treat you."

"And what about *you*? What will *you* wear?"

Nora could tell that Emma hadn't expected she would be part of the experiment.

"I'll go upstairs and get you some of *my* non-pink sweaters," Nora said, glad to see that Emma was starting to look nervous, too. "And you can see how *you* feel and how other people act toward *you*."

Then Emma's face brightened.

"This can be—"

No. Emma couldn't be serious.

"—our science-fair project!" Emma concluded.

"We can't do a science-fair project on how people feel about the color pink!"

"Why not? Remember the project in Coach Joe's

126

book about how people feel about different kinds of animals?"

The one that Nora had already rejected as hopelessly dumb?

"Look," Emma said. "To make it more scientific, we'll take a survey in class at the end of the week to see what people noticed. Surveys are scientific. You can make graphs about the results. Graphs

are scientific. And we can keep a journal of our feelings. That's sort of scientific."

"*Feelings* aren't *scientific*," Nora insisted.

"Who says they're not?" Emma shot back. "Why can't scientists study feelings the way they'd study anything else?"

Emma had a point. But no science-fair judge would think that a sweater-trading project was worthy of selection for the regional science fair.

And yet . . . Nora *was* curious to see what she and Emma would find out.

And it wasn't as if they had any better idea, or any other idea at all.

And in the end, curiosity—the deep-down desire to figure something out—was what true science was all about.

Nora's mother noticed first.

"Where did you get that sweater?" she asked Monday morning as she handed Nora a plate of scrambled eggs and toast for breakfast.

"I borrowed it from Emma."

The puzzlement on her mother's face gave way to good-natured amusement.

"So that's starting," she said. "I remember sharing outfits with my best friend, but I don't think we got into clothes that way until middle school."

Nora forced a smile. She had decided not to tell her parents about the new idea for the science-fair project; in fact, with all the commotion over Nellie's arrival, she had never told them the curling-iron idea, either. The whole point of the new experiment was to see how people reacted when they didn't know it *was* an experiment. But it was strange to have her very own mother treat her as the kind of girl who was "into" clothes.

At school that morning, Nora expected pink fireworks to explode all around her, with the other girls crowding up to her to exclaim, "Nora! You're wearing pink! Look, everybody! Nora is wearing pink!"

That didn't happen.

Amy did say, "Nice sweater, Nora. Is it new?" And Nora thought she read a question in Amy's eyes. Tamara nodded in agreement with the compliment, and that was that. Busy talking over every detail of Saturday's party, the other girls didn't seem to notice either Emma's plain sweater or Nora's pink-pink-pink one.

Mason and Brody, sitting next to Nora in the huddle, said nothing about the unusual hue of her clothes. Dunk plopped himself down next to Emma the way he always did, showing her how he could make rude noises with a hand cupped under his armpit. Emma reacted as she always did: she giggled.

"All right, team!" Coach Joe said, calling the huddle to order. "How have you all been making out on the Oregon Trail? Any Indian raids? Any outbreaks of cholera? Any snakebites to report? Who's willing to share?"

Nora had written a new diary entry last night, a long observation by Martha Talbot about moose, ending with her now-standard sign-off: "Baby crying! Must go!"

Emma volunteered to read from her diary about Ann Whittaker, the independent woman off to seek her fortune on the trail, the plucky woman who would open the first school in the Oregon Territory, the person whose fate card should have been assigned to Nora instead.

Dear Diary,

We have reached Kansas. The trail only goes across a little corner of Kansas, but there are sunflowers everywhere. When I start my school in Oregon, I'm going to have my students write poems about sunflowers. If sunflowers grow in Oregon. If not, they can write poems about whatever flowers grow there. I will put all of the poems into a special class book.

Emma stopped reading and said to Coach Joe, "If you want to borrow that idea, go right ahead."

"Thanks, Emma," Coach Joe said with a grin. "Is there anything else happening to Ann right now in Kansas?"

"Oh, *yes*," Emma said. She resumed reading.

There is a fellow on the trail named Dave Edwin. I think he's sweet on me.

Amy rolled her eyes at Nora as Bethy, Elise, and Tamara started giggling. The name Dave Edwin certainly sounded a lot like Dunk Edwards. Emma tried to shush the gigglers with a glare, but then she started giggling, too.

He picked a bunch of sunflowers and gave them to me. I put them in a vase inside my wagon. I don't think a fellow would give flowers to a girl if he didn't like her, do you, dear Diary?

Now Dave is waiting to go for a walk with me in the moonlight. So I'm going to put on my prettiest shawl and go.

Bye for now.

Love,
Ann

"The plot thickens," Coach Joe said with another grin.

"Coach Joe?" Emma asked now that she had gotten her giggles under control. "If Ann is a schoolteacher, can she still—well—get married?"

Coach Joe thought for a moment before replying. "Back then, there were few professions open

132

to women. Teaching was one of the only ones. And as far as I know, only single women taught school. They gave up teaching after they married."

Emma's face fell. Nora could tell that Emma still didn't like the future written on Ann's fate card.

"In any case," Coach Joe said, "we're looking forward to the next installment of Ann's story, aren't we, team?"

Next Amy read her dramatic scene about saving her baby from the rattlesnake. Nora noticed she had some details wrong. The rattlesnake wouldn't have been six feet long, more like three or four. And its rattling would not have been as loud as thunder! But she didn't say anything. She had learned back in kindergarten that nobody liked a know-it-all, and Amy had definitely made the scene exciting.

One more kid read. And then the huddle was over.

"What are we supposed to be doing now?" Nora whispered to Emma as science time began. "We can't talk about our project because no one is allowed to know about it. But we can't spend science time doing absolutely nothing."

"We can still talk about curling irons," Emma said, "and I can imagine how happy I would have been if my parents had let me get a bunch of new ones. Coach Joe doesn't know yet that the project fell through."

"Coach Joe doesn't know what?"

Nora hadn't heard the teacher come up behind them.

"It's a secret," Emma said, "but it's a good secret, and it has to do with the science fair, and you'll find out on Friday when everybody else does."

Emma was definitely good at dealing with the unexpected.

"Is everything all right in the land of curling irons?" he asked them.

"Oh, yes!" Emma said. "We're learning ever so much!"

"Well," Coach Joe said, with an approving smile, "I'm glad you two have managed to work so well together. Nora, I'm especially proud of you for being willing to take on a whole new ball game, really stretch and grow as a player."

He was about to head over to another pod when his eyes fell again on Nora in her pink sweater. "New uniform?" he asked, with another smile—amused this time, as her mother's smile had been that morning.

Coach Joe was a very noticing teacher.

Nora didn't say anything, but she felt herself flushing. It was odd to have her clothes commented on. Did Coach Joe think it was a good thing that she had not only a whole new ball game but a new uniform to go with it?

She wasn't used to wondering what people thought of her based on what she had decided to wear.

At home that evening, washing her hands before another hastily assembled dinner of leftover take-out, Nora caught a glimpse in the bathroom mirror of a pretty girl in a soft pink sweater that matched her glowing pink cheeks.

Was that her?

Apparently, it was.

A baby's head is 1/4 the size of its total body length, compared to 1/8 for adults. So no wonder it's so heavy that a baby's neck needs supporting. But I still can't believe you can break a baby just by holding its neck a teensy bit wrong.

On Tuesday, Nora wore a different pink sweater of Emma's. This one was puffier and rufflier, with bows on the sleeves. No one in her family made any further comments about her choice of clothing, because Sarah's husband, Jeff, had gotten his leave approved and would be home to meet his brand-new daughter that afternoon. The color of Nora's sweater was the last thing on anybody's mind.

And at lunch, the girls were talking about how unfair it was that Dunk was getting away with doing nothing on the science-fair project he was supposed to be working on with Sheng. Poor Sheng had to do everything. Even Emma agreed that Dunk was lazy.

"You know, I'm just as glad I'm not Martha Talbot," Emma said, looking sympathetically at Nora. "I'm not sure I'd want to be married to Tom Talbot. Not when Dave Edwin is bringing me flowers all the time to decorate my covered wagon."

That got everyone talking about the Oregon Trail documentary that was going to be filmed on Friday, the same day as the science fair.

"For my prop, I'm going to bring in sunflowers, of course," Emma said. "The ones from Dave Edwin."

"I'm going to bring in my grandmother's butter churn," Elise said. "She has a real old-time butter churn, not that she's ever churned butter in it. It's just for show. She said I could borrow it for the movie."

"Nora, you're bringing Nellie, right?" Emma remembered to ask.

This produced a chorus of pleading.

"Bring her!"

"Bring her!"

"Bring her!"

But this time, Nora wasn't going to make any promises she didn't know for a fact she could keep.

"Maybe" was all Nora said. "I'll try."

During that afternoon's huddle, Mason read his latest diary entry as Jake Smith.

Dear Diary,

Do you want to know what's not fun?

I'll tell you what's not fun.

Gathering a couple of bushels of dried buffalo dung is not fun.

In case you didn't know, dung is another word for poop.

Why, you may ask, am I collecting buffalo poop? Because here in the middle of Nowhere, Wyoming, it's all we have for fuel. No trees. No sticks. No anything. So we burn dried buffalo dung.

Did I mention that dung doesn't smell so great when it burns? And it burns fast, which is why we have to gather so much of it.

Oh, and guess what we cook with all this dung? Beans, bacon, and biscuits. Every single day.

Now, I happen to like eating the same things every single day.

Just not these things.

Yours truly,
Jake Smith

Coach Joe's class hooted and hollered for that one. They always laughed at any mention of bodily waste products, which Nora thought was silly. But it was Mason's melancholy tone of voice when he read that made her laugh, too.

"Cheer up, Jake," Coach Joe said. He pointed to the large map of the Oregon Trail route hanging on the wall in the huddle corner of the room. "You're almost to Oregon, where you'll live off the fat of the land in peace and prosperity."

"But I haven't even crossed the mountains yet," Mason protested. "Or reached the Snake River— nice name. Or met up with the really enormous mosquitoes. Believe me, the worst is yet to come."

Nora laughed again. "The worst is yet to come" was definitely Mason's motto.

"Well, keep us all posted," Coach Joe said with a chuckle.

After the huddle, Nora had time to ask Mason and Brody, "So *does* it? *Does* toast fall more often butter-side down?"

"Maybe a little bit more often," Brody said. "We dropped thirty pieces of toast, and seventeen times it fell butter-side down and thirteen times it fell butter-side up. So I guess we proved something."

"But not a very big something," Mason put in. "What we really proved is that if a dog eats thirty pieces of buttered toast, he'll throw up all over the family-room carpet, and the kids who dropped the toast are the ones who get stuck cleaning it up."

Nora burst out laughing, and Mason and Brody both laughed with her.

When Nora arrived home from school, a tall, smiling man with close-cropped light hair met her at the door and swung her up into a hug.

"Auntie Nora!" he greeted her. "Aunt to the cutest, sweetest niece in the world!"

Nora grinned at Jeff, and Jeff grinned back. Then he looked at her again, puzzled. "Did you do something different to your hair?"

Nora shook her head. She would never do anything different to her hair. Maybe the pink sweater
made everything about her seem altered somehow.

From the couch, nursing Nellie, Sarah beamed
the biggest smile Nora had seen from her sister
since before Nellie was born.

"I can stay for a week," Jeff said. "Not long enough to teach Nellie to throw my famous curveball, but enough to warm up her pitching arm, at least. And then, come June, I'll be home for good."

Sarah radiated so much happiness at Jeff's return that it seemed a good time for Nora to ask her question.

"Some of the girls are wondering—" she began.

"Not another party!" Sarah said, but she sounded amused, not annoyed.

"No, but on Friday we're having the science fair in the morning—"

Sarah's face darkened. "Nora, I already said that you're not using Nellie for the science fair."

Nora glared at Sarah for not letting her finish.

"And we're making this documentary about the Oregon Trail in the afternoon. We each play an Oregon Trail person, and my person is named Martha Talbot. She's a mom with three kids, and one of them is a newborn baby. Everyone is bringing in props for the movie, and so I thought maybe Nellie—"

"*Nellie* is not a *prop*!" Sarah said.

"Well, not a prop, exactly, but—"

"A co-star!" Jeff helped her out. "You want to know if Nellie can co-star in her first movie, is that right? Will Sarah and I get a share of the profits? So we can afford to send her to baseball camp when she's older?"

Nora knew Jeff was joking.

"What do you say, Sarah?" Jeff asked. "Sounds okay to me, if one of us is there with her."

"Okay," Sarah said. "Nellie may come to school on Friday."

"Thanks!" Nora said to both of them, but especially to Jeff.

Now was not the time to tell Jeff that Nellie wasn't going to *baseball* camp someday, but to *science* camp. Anyway, there was no reason Nellie couldn't do both. Nora herself liked science and basketball. Nellie could also like more than one thing.

Nellie might even be a baseball-playing scientist who—sometimes—wore pink?

On Thursday, Coach Joe let Nora and Emma hand out a survey in the afternoon. The survey had only one question on it: "Did you notice anything different about Emma and Nora this week?" They had deliberately not mentioned clothes in the question to avoid biasing the answers.

Nora pounced on the collected surveys right before the dismissal bell.

Of the thirteen boys in the class, not one had noticed anything about their clothes. Only one boy had noticed anything to do with them at all. Dunk had noticed that Emma was being mean to him!

Nora wondered if Dunk had any clue why Emma had stopped giggling every time he burped during a huddle or jostled her in the lunch line. Had he figured out that Emma preferred the attentions of a male who would bring her prairie sunflowers and help yoke up the oxen that pulled her covered wagon? Even if that male had the drawback of being imaginary?

Of the eleven other girls in their class, most had noticed nothing at all. Amy and Tamara both wrote, "Nora got some new sweaters"; neither commented that the sweaters were pink. Not a single girl said anything about Emma's having worn Nora's plain, dark sweaters for four days in a row, except for Bethy, who wrote, "Something seemed a little strange about Emma this week, but I'm not sure what."

That was all! So did that prove nobody knew or cared whether you wore pink or blue? Was Nora right that clothes didn't matter? The survey somehow didn't capture how strange Nora had felt when her mother thought she was "into" clothes, and Jeff asked if she had a new hairdo, and Coach Joe praised her new "uniform," and she saw her pink self in the mirror.

It was hard to study feelings.

Nora stuffed the surveys in her backpack and hurried to join Amy in the dismissal line. Amy's mother was picking them up for their volunteer work at the animal shelter. Then, after supper, Nora was going to Emma's house to spend the evening doing what they could to salvage the science fair, which was tomorrow.

Tomorrow!

All they had was some scribbled surveys and random feelings. What kind of science-fair experiment was that?

Nora knew the answer: not much of one at all.

At the shelter, Brad gave them a friendly hello. He was busy chatting with a co-worker at the front desk, an older man whose name tag identified him as Bob.

Brad brought out the first pair of dogs for the girls to walk: a frisky Lab named Bailey and a smaller dog of uncertain breed named Taffy. It was an unseasonably warm day, so warm that Nora shed her jacket.

"Be careful with Bailey," Brad told Amy. "He can be a handful." He reached past Nora to hand Bailey's leash to Amy.

"Taffy's a little sweetheart," he told Nora.

As the girls led the dogs outdoors, Mrs. Talia trailing behind, Nora asked Amy, "So which color seed do parakeets like best?"

"The brighter the better! They definitely went straight for orange and yellow, because those were the brightest," Amy said. "Maybe because their feathers are so bright, it makes them want to eat foods that match?"

That seemed far-fetched to Nora, but she could believe that bright colors might catch a bird's eye.

"What was the point of the survey?" Amy asked Nora then. "Asking if anybody noticed anything different about you and Emma?"

Nora hadn't yet told Amy anything about the curling-iron fiasco and Emma's new idea; there was no reason not to tell her now, as the survey results were already in. But she still felt too discouraged about the whole thing to admit what had happened, even to Amy.

"All will be revealed tomorrow!" Nora said, with more enthusiasm than she felt. "It has to do with the science fair." Then she added, "With our very bad and awful project."

"I told you the curling-iron idea isn't bad and awful!"

"Well, something happened with the curling irons. So we had to switch ideas. And the new idea is really bad. I mean, really bad. But all will be revealed tomorrow," Nora said again, this time with a sigh.

"Okay," Amy said, sounding hurt.

The next two dogs were a Chihuahua for Nora and a husky for Amy, and then Nora walked a sweet, half-blind sheepdog while Amy strained to hold on to the leash of a sleek greyhound.

The girls had fallen silent, Amy apparently miffed at being left out of Nora's science-fair secrets, Nora still trying to figure out how to turn Emma's idea into something that wouldn't be the lamest science-fair project in the whole fourth grade.

Did clothes matter?

The surveys, for the most part, said no. That meant Nora had been right.

But there was something about how everyone had treated Nora all week that might mean Emma was right.

"Harley, slow down!" Amy called to her dog as Nora's old, gentle dog continued to lumber along a few steps behind.

A thought popped into Nora's always-curious brain.

And then another thought.

And another.

Thoughts that might lead to a science-fair break-through.

Or not.

"Amy," she said, "do you think we can stay a lit-tle bit longer today, or does your mom have to pick up Sheridan right away?"

"My dad's getting Sheridan. Why?"

"Would you be willing to do an experiment with me? It's connected with the science fair, and I'll tell you about everything in a minute, I promise I will, but first I have to see if I'm right about something."

"Um, sure," Amy said, already starting to tug on her braid, fastened with plain rubber bands today.

Nora looked down at Amy's army camouflage jacket, as different as could be from the flouncy pink sweater of Emma's that Nora was wearing.

"And will you trade clothes with me? Wear my sweater for a little while and let me wear your jacket?"

"Nora, now you're being weird," Amy said.

"I'm not being weird," Nora told Amy, her heart beating as fast as a newborn baby's. "I'm being scientific."

The typical girl baby will speak her first word about a month earlier than the typical boy baby. Girl babies are also about a month ahead of boys, on average, in the number of words they understand. But the difference here is tiny. Lots of boys start to talk early, and lots of girls start to talk late.

The Plainfield Elementary science fair was held all over the school, with projects on display in the gym, in the library, and along the hallway leading from one to the other.

Coach Joe's students, their projects arrayed atop the low bookcases in the library, were the oddest-looking group of scientists Nora had ever seen. In her day, she had definitely seen some peculiar astrophysicists at her mother's conferences and strange biochemists at conferences she tagged along to with her father. But she had never seen female scientists wearing gingham pioneer dresses complete with aprons and sunbonnets. Or male scientists who looked like they had dressed up as cowboys for Halloween.

Maybe it hadn't been the best idea to film the Oregon Trail documentary on the same day as the science fair.

Nora owned one faded pioneer-looking dress and one droopy sunbonnet. She'd left the sunbonnet in Coach Joe's classroom, but there was nothing she could do about the dress.

Emma had on a bright pink Southern-belle dress with a hoopskirt and a matching pink parasol. In Nora's opinion, Emma's outfit was completely ridiculous for a pioneer woman traveling on her own over a thousand miles of wilderness, from Missouri to Oregon, who had to do all the same backbreaking chores as any man on the trail.

On the other hand, Nora could see how Emma's outfit might well make a fellow feel like bringing her some flowers and then sticking around to chop her firewood and haul her water from the nearest creek. The big bunch of sunflowers Emma had brought to school was back on Emma's desk.

What would the science-fair judges think when they came by to question them about their project?

Oh well. The whole point of the project was to figure out how people reacted to other people's choice of clothing. And if Nora was right, they had now proved something, they really had.

Standing next to Emma, Nora read over the information on their three-panel display board once again. "The Power of Pink" was the title Emma had come up with. Nora thought it was a dumb title. But she didn't think the results were dumb.

On the board, she and Emma had displayed a blue pie chart showing that 100 percent of the boys had noticed nothing, and a pink pie chart showing that only two and a half out of eleven girls (they counted Bethy as half), or 23 percent, had noticed anything. The girls had also mounted a picture of Nora, unsmiling, in Emma's pink sweater, and a picture of Emma, smiling, in Nora's dark blue one. They'd also posted a few of the responses to the survey question, "Did you notice anything different about Emma and Nora this week?":

"No."

155

"Nope."

"Like what?"

"No."

"No."

"No."

But then they'd added the results that Nora and Amy had found out the day before. On their two visits to the animal shelter, they had each walked a total of ten dogs, three on the first day and seven yesterday, to test Nora's new hypothesis. The first day, when Amy had worn a pink jacket and pink ribbons on her braids and Nora had worn her usual dark sweater, Brad had given bigger dogs to Nora and smaller dogs to Amy. The next time, when Nora had worn Emma's sweater and Amy had worn her army jacket, Brad had given bigger dogs to Amy and smaller dogs to Nora. Later on, when they had switched clothes and Bob had taken over at the desk to hand out leashes, three out of four times he gave the girl wearing pink a smaller, easier dog to walk.

Nora knew it wasn't a big sample. And there were so many other variables to consider. But they had still found out something. People (at least two different people making dog-walking assignments) gave smaller and easier dogs (at least most of the time on those two days) to girls wearing pink.

Sheng and Dunk's project—well, Sheng's project—was displayed right next to Nora and Emma's. Mason and Brody's falling-toast exhibit (they had managed to include a cute picture of Dog grabbing one piece) was far away, by the little-kid picture books. Amy and Anthony were practically out in the hall, with their dyed birdseed arrayed in front of their poster in little bowls.

Nora studied Sheng's display board: "Turning Potential Energy into Kinetic Energy." It had graphs galore. It had equations. No pictures of girls wearing sweaters, no fancy Emma stenciling, no pink-flower decals that Emma had added when Nora wasn't paying attention.

But maybe graphs and equations weren't everything?

Nora's parents both had to work, but a few parents stopped by to admire or ask questions, as well as lots of kids from other grades, who seemed more interested in Emma's parasol than in reading the content of their display.

Dunk abandoned his own project to come look at theirs, except that he didn't seem to be looking at theirs at all. He had gone back to Coach Joe's classroom and returned with something held behind his back that he didn't seem to want them to see.

"What do *you* want?" Emma asked him, in the same cool tone she had been using for the past few days.

"Nothing," Dunk said.

"What are you hiding there?"

"Nothing," Dunk said again.

Then he held out a tin can filled with sunflowers.

As Emma stared, Dunk plopped the sunflowers on the table next to Nora and Emma's science-fair display and hurried away to the other side of the library.

Emma gave a romantic sigh.

So maybe boys gave flowers more often to girls who wore pink? That would be a science-fair project for another day.

A moment later, Dunk was back, with a hopeful look on his face. Emma welcomed him with a smile.

Encouraged, Dunk snatched her parasol. She tussled with him to get it back.

He grunted. She giggled.

Apparently, Dave Edwin's sunflowers were forgotten, wilting in a faraway imaginary wagon.

Ten minutes later, the judges appeared, a man and a woman carrying clipboards. Sometimes the judges were somebody's mom or dad, but sometimes they were real scientists. And of course, sometimes they were both. Nora's dad had been a judge last year.

"Tell us about your project," the female judge prompted.

"The first thing you need to know is that Nora and I didn't want to be partners," Emma said. "Coach Joe made us all keep our regular science partners, whether we wanted to or not. I'm not being mean. I'm just stating a fact."

Nora believed in stating facts. But this particular fact was a strange one to share with the judges.

"And Nora and I could not come up with an idea!" Emma went on. "Nora likes ants! And batteries!

And I don't even like science at all! But then I went to Nora's house because she has the cutest new baby niece, and Nora was mad because everybody kept buying Nellie pink things, and I said that I felt prettier when I wore pink, and that other people thought I looked prettier, too, and Nora said that was dumb—"

"I didn't say it was dumb," Nora put in. Well, now that she thought back to the day of the party, that was exactly what she had said.

"You *did*, Nora, and we got into this big discussion of whether clothes mattered or not, and we decided to test it. Scientifically. And we were both right. Nora was right that when we changed clothes for a week, and she wore pink and I wore not-pink, hardly anybody noticed."

Emma finally paused, in evident amazement at these findings, and Nora took over.

"But then when another friend and I were volunteering to walk dogs at the animal shelter, the people in charge kept giving bigger, rougher dogs to whichever one of us wasn't wearing pink. I started tabulating the data, and this is what we found." She pointed to the chart that displayed the dog-walking results. "So maybe Emma was right that people react differently to clothes color, even if they don't realize that's what they're doing."

Both the man judge and the woman judge were busy scribbling notes.

"Do you think your classmates would have noticed if you had come to school wearing . . . *that*?" the man asked, gesturing toward Emma's dress.

"Maybe," Emma said. "But both Nora and I wore *normal*-looking clothes, except that Nora wore normal-looking clothes for *me*, and I wore normal-looking clothes for *her*. But they were still *normal*."

"Do you think your project gives a reason for girls to avoid wearing pink?" the woman asked.

"No!" Emma said. "Who cares what kind of dog you walk? *I* don't."

"No," Nora echoed, more tentatively. "We didn't have time to show anything that definite. But maybe we showed that it's good for all of us to pay attention to whether we judge other people on things that don't really matter."

Were what colors you wore a part of your fate? When people reacted to you differently because of

161

those colors, did it make you start to *be* someone different?

If Nora had worn pink every day of her life, would she now act more like Emma? If Emma had never worn pink, would she now act more like Nora?

Maybe there were some things even science would have a hard time figuring out.

The judges moved on to Sheng and Dunk. Nora could hear Sheng's long, detailed description of "their" experiment. Dunk said nothing. Instead, as Sheng talked on, he grabbed Emma's parasol and opened it over his own head.

"Dunk," the man judge interrupted him. "Tell us about why the two of you decided to study kinetic energy."

Dunk shrugged, but he did shut Emma's parasol.

"Do you think your experiment suggested any other questions you might want to explore next?" the woman judge asked.

"Not really," Dunk replied, still holding on to Emma's parasol as she fake-glared at him to give it back.

"Thanks, boys," both judges said to Dunk and Sheng, and went on to the next exhibit.

"I think they liked ours!" Emma said to Nora, once the judges were out of earshot.

Nora hoped Emma was right.

"But we only had two charts," Nora couldn't help pointing out.

"Graphs, schmaphs!" Emma returned. "Ours was *interesting*! Ours showed something that people really want to *know*. Dunk, give me my parasol!"

Emma reached for it.

Dunk held it high over his head.

Emma giggled.

Babies like to be rocked around 70 movements per minute, about the same rhythm as a parent's beating heart.

15

Coach Joe gave out instructions for the filming of the class Oregon Trail documentary in an after-lunch huddle. He was dressed in an Oregon Trail outfit himself, or at least a cowboy outfit, complete with leather chaps, a bright red bandanna around his neck, and a ten-gallon hat.

"We're going to film the interviews right here in our classroom," he said. "I had hoped for a quiet corner of the library, but with the science fair going on all day, there's no quiet corner anywhere. I'll be the interviewer, asking each of you a couple

164

of questions for you to answer in character. So this afternoon, I'm not Coach Joe; I'm Ace Reporter Joe, covering the Oregon Trail for the *Westward-Bound Times*. Tamara's dad volunteered to film us and edit the tapes into our final project; he's made a few indie films himself. And I'll need all of you to be a quiet, respectful audience while we film. Got it?"

Everyone nodded. Nora wasn't sure Dunk could manage being quiet and respectful, but the thought of being in a real film made by a real filmmaker had caused a hush to fall over everyone, Dunk included.

"Okay, team," Coach Joe said, concluding the huddle. "Lights! Camera! Action!"

Seated at her desk, Nora tuned out during some of the interviews, quietly reading her new library book on the scientist Marie Curie, but she tuned back in for the kids she knew best.

Ace Reporter Joe to Emma Averill/Ann Whittaker:
What is the biggest challenge you've faced on the trail so far?

Emma/Ann: Maybe this sounds dumb, but I have to wash my hair in cold water from a nasty creek, and that wouldn't matter so much except that there's this fellow who's sweet on me. Well, actually two fellows. It's sort of complicated. Anyway, they both brought me sunflowers. Aren't they pretty? So I want to look halfway decent! And you try looking halfway decent when you have to wash your hair in a creek five hundred miles from anywhere!

Ace Reporter Joe to Brody Baxter/Bill Breeden: What hardships have you been encountering on your journey?

Brody/Bill: It's been great! My dog, Pup, loves chasing prairie dogs and rabbits. He's probably the best prairie-dog-and-rabbit chaser ever in the history of the Oregon Trail. A lot of the people on the trip are complaining about the weather, you know, because of the tornado and the hailstorm. But the tornado missed us! It went right by! And the hailstorm was exciting, except that Pup got scared, and the hail punched a bunch of holes in the cover of my wagon. But I *like* the holes because I get more of a breeze that way!

Ace Reporter Joe to Mason Dixon/Jake Smith: So a little bird told me things have been going pretty well for you. Is that correct?

Mason/Jake: It's been going great *if* you like bouncing along in a boiling-hot wagon over huge ruts all day long. And cooking all your food—or what the people around here call food—over stinky buffalo chips. And did the little bird tell you about the tornado? And the hailstorm? And don't even get me started on the mosquitoes!

Ace Reporter Joe to Amy Talia/Sally Hamilton: You're the heroine of the trail, Mrs. Hamilton, for your quick thinking about that rattlesnake. Can you tell me about it?

Amy/Sally: Well, it was definitely a huge, scary snake. Four feet long! And it had this really quiet, deadly rattle. But all I could think about was my poor little baby, so I ran over to the rattler with my hatchet, and whack-whack-whack, that was the last time that snake was going to bother anybody!

Nora had been unable to resist correcting Amy's rattlesnake facts. She was glad Amy could still make a thrilling story with a shorter, quieter snake. Facts didn't spoil stories, in her opinion; they made them even better.

Nora saw Sarah, Jeff, and Nellie standing in the doorway of the classroom.

"Nora, let's film you next," Coach Joe said; Nora had told him Nellie was on her way.

Slowly Nora walked to the corner where Coach Joe sat on one stool, leaving a second stool for his interviewee. She adjusted her sunbonnet to stall for time.

In less than a minute—in thirty seconds—she was going to have to hold Nellie again, on camera this time, filmed for posterity.

Nellie was dressed not in a twenty-first-century stretchy sleeper, but in a little cotton dress that could have been worn by a pioneer baby. On Nellie's head was a little sunbonnet that matched Nora's.

"Here." Jeff held Nellie out to Nora.

Nora hesitated.

"What?" Jeff asked.

Sarah flushed.

"Nora," she said in a low voice. "I shouldn't have freaked out at the party. It's just been . . . so hard. I've always been good at being a geologist, and I thought, *How hard can it be to be a mom?* But it's much harder than I thought it would be; there's so much that you can't learn in advance, however many books you read. Being a mom is scary! But I shouldn't have acted the way I did with you."

Sarah gathered her into a hug; gratefully, Nora hugged her back.

Being an aunt was scary, too.

She still felt nervous about holding Nellie.

But then she thought: *Nora Alpers might not know how to hold a baby.*

But Martha Talbot does.

Perched on her stool, she let Sarah settle Nellie into her arms. She held Nellie close against her chest, the way Martha Talbot would, careful to support Nellie's little neck.

She could hear the girls give a collective sigh of envy. What was a butter churn as a prop—or even a double bunch of sunflowers—compared to an actual baby?

169

Don't cry, Nora/Martha silently pleaded with Nellie.

Nellie didn't. She snuggled deeper.

Ace Reporter Joe to Nora Alpers/Martha Talbot: How are you faring on the Oregon Trail?

Nora/Martha: All right, I guess.

What a boring answer! Emma, Brody, Mason, and Amy had all done better than that!

Ace Reporter Joe: Anything else you'd like to share?

Nora/Martha: I like seeing new kinds of wildlife everywhere.

She tried to remember some of her diary entries.

Nora/Martha: Especially crows. Did you know that crows have the biggest brain-to-body ratio of all bird species?

Ace Reporter Joe: So it sounds as if looking after a husband and three little ones hasn't kept you from making lots of scientific observations, Mrs. Talbot. Good for you!

That was the end of the interview. Sarah took Nellie back from Nora, Nora gave her sister a parting hug, and Sarah, Jeff, and Nellie slipped away.

Back at her desk again, Nora thought about Ace Reporter Joe's last comment. Although she had signed every diary entry by writing, "Baby crying! Gotta go!" she hadn't written anything else about her family at all.

Despite being a busy mother of three, she had written about science.

Despite being a single woman alone, Emma had found herself a beau.

Destined to die of a fever in Wyoming, Brody had been his sunny, happy self.

Destined to live a long and prosperous life in Oregon, Mason had done nothing but complain.

Whatever the fate cards had said, without any trading of fate cards along the way, all of them had remained true to themselves.

Nora still didn't know where those selves came from.

Maybe there was some kind of fate card that the laws of science gave you at birth? Maybe how other people treated you every day for all kinds of strange reasons was a fate card of its own?

Or maybe not.

There was a lot, she realized, that she didn't know about fate.

The Plainfield Elementary PA system clicked on ten minutes before the dismissal bell.

Nora heard the voice of the principal, who was getting ready to announce the results of the science-fair judging: which four projects from each grade had been selected for the regional science fair at the university next month.

Nora couldn't block the thought: If only she could have done a really scientific science-fair project, by herself and not with Emma!

Then again, she and Emma had found out something pretty interesting she would never have learned otherwise.

The principal read the names of the winners from the lower grades.

Then: "Fourth grade. 'Slope Angle and Erosion,' by Alice Eaton and Bryant Quinley." Two kids not in Coach Joe's class.

"'Turning Potential Energy into Kinetic Energy.'"

"That's us!" Dunk shouted, pumping his fist into the air. "We won!"

"By Sheng Ji," the principal's voice continued.

"Wait! He forgot to say my name!" Dunk said.

But Nora knew that the principal hadn't *forgotten* to say Dunk's name. The judges must have left it off the prize on purpose.

Dunk reddened as he realized that, too. Despite her earlier comments about his laziness, Emma clucked indignantly on his behalf and took a sympathetic sniff of his sunflowers in the tin can on her desk.

The principal was still reading out project names. "'Judging Sound by Direction,' by Latisha Jones and Eric Chu." Two other kids not in Coach Joe's class.

"'The Power of Pink,' by Nora Alpers and Emma Averill."

That couldn't be right. Not with that dumb title

that Emma had insisted on. Not with only two charts!

Emma squealed and threw herself at Nora for a hug.

"That's *us*!"

Stunned, Nora hugged Emma back.

At home, Nora checked on her ant farm. She didn't want her ants to think she had forgotten them in all the excitement of the science fair, the Oregon Trail, and a brand-new niece. Not that her ants knew or cared whether she remembered them or not, so long as food and water arrived every day.

She saw a new branched tunnel near where an old tunnel had collapsed. Two ants were struggling to carry off the morsel of cracker she had deposited in the farm as today's allotment of food.

Despite everything, ants were still ants, and always would be.

Nora found Sarah and Jeff upstairs in the guest room, changing Nellie.

"Thanks for bringing her to school today," Nora told them.

"Don't forget to give us our cut of the box-office take for the movie," Jeff joked.

Nellie wasn't wearing her pioneer dress; she had on another sleeper, not pink this time but pale green with yellow stripes.

"Can I hold her again?" Nora asked.

"Sure. She's clean and dry now," Sarah said.

Nora perched on the edge of Sarah's unmade bed, holding Nellie the way Martha Talbot had held her before. It was less scary holding a baby for the third time.

Nora said in a low voice, "Hi, Nellie. I'm your aunt Nora."

Nellie gurgled with contentment.

"And I'm going to teach you all about science."

The baby looked ready to fall asleep. Science lessons would have to wait. But for now, at least, Nora could sing Nellie a lullaby.

"The ants go marching one by one, hurrah, hurrah!" Nora sang as softly as she could.

Eyes closed, Nellie gave a sigh of appreciation.

"The ants go marching two by two, hurrah, hurrah!" Nora whispered.

A baby only 10 days old can already tell the difference between her mother's smell and someone else's. I wonder how long it takes for a baby to recognize her aunt's smell, too.

ACKNOWLEDGMENTS

I'm always grateful whenever I'm given the chance to express gratitude. My wonderful editor, Nancy Hinkel, makes each email exchange and phone call a delight: what a gift she has for bringing the best out of every story. Katie Kath's illustrations for the book couldn't be more adorable. Thanks also to my constantly supportive agent, Steve Fraser; to fabulously careful copy editors Karen Sherman, Janet Renard, Amy Schroeder, and Artie Bennett; to Isabel Warren-Lynch and Trish Parcell for their appealing book design; and to Stephen Brown and Julia Maguire for help throughout in countless ways. Above all, I'm grateful to Kataleya Lee Wahl, the most important baby in my life, who is truly never any trouble at all.

ABOUT THE AUTHOR

Claudia Mills is the author of over fifty books for young readers, including the Mason Dixon series. She does not personally keep an ant farm, but she does have a cat, Snickers, with whom she curls up on her couch at home in Boulder, Colorado, drinking hot chocolate and writing. Visit her at claudiamillsauthor.com.